There comes a time in all our lives when we
pause to say,

"I Wish I Had Waited".

Contact Information:
Letts Dream Big Publishing
P. O. Box 472172
Garland, TX 75047-2172
lettsdreambigpublishing@comcast.net
www.lettsdreambigpublishing.com

Special Acknowledgements

My husband, Michael, thank you for all your love and support. You have put my writing above your golf career time and time again. Your day will come to shine and I know you will.

My children, Michael II and Courtney, you guys have been wonderful. You leave me in peace when you know I need to finish a project. You guys rock!

My mother, Mattie Willis has always supported me in my writing endeavors. You told me this would be the one. I'm holding you to it Mama.

Thanks to my mother-in-law, Lorna Lett who was willing to put her money where her mouth was. She's my partner in Letts Dream Big Publishing.

A special thank you to Shauna Lett for the awesome book cover. I gave you my vision and you ran with it like the artist you are. I'm sure this is only the beginning for you.

I have an awesome support team in my wonderful siblings, Earl, Johnnie, Liz, Val, Sam and Bessie. You guys encouraged me to follow my dream of writing.

To my teen reviewers, Heather, Tamara, and Christina, thank you for your input. You asked me to make the book longer and I ran with it. I tried to keep it real for you guys and I think I succeeded.

Thank you adult reviewers as well. I guess I should have warned your there would be a few tears.

To all my online writing buddies thanks for your support and encouragement. You guys have been great and I've learned a lot from you.

Author, Shelia Goss thank you for all the publishing tips. I would have been lost without you!

Thank you GS Service Unit 146 for your continued support.

Chapter 1
Memory Lane

Rainey winced with each step she took up the tree house ladder. Her whole body ached as she eased onto the platform at last. She opened the door and crawled through the small space.

She let out a blood-curdling scream when a flashlight beamed in her face. Her heart raced as she stared at her childhood friends, Tamara and Alicia.

She hadn't spoken to either of them in months. When they did speak, it was only in passing. They were once best friends.

Over the years the three of them drifted apart and by the time they reached 9th grade, they each had gone their separate ways. They all had other interests and other friends.

"What are you two doing here?" She asked placing her hand over her still pounding heart. She breathed in deeply to help calm her already frazzled nerves.

Her day had suddenly gone from bad to worse if that were possible. She was not in the right frame of mind to deal with either of them.

"It's a free country," Alicia snapped turning off her flashlight. She pulled her cap down to shield her face from prying eyes. Her fingers nervously fingered the thin gold cross around her throat. She gripped the cross so tight, it left an indention in her palm.

"I live here. This is my father's property and I think you both should leave," Tamara voiced also turning off her flashlight. "You are not welcome here anymore, either one of you. I suggest you both leave before I call the police and have you arrested for trespassing. Although it would be a new experience for Alicia, Rainey I'm sure you don't need anything more added to your rap sheet. Out of curiosity does Zeke have you robbing liquor stores yet?"

"A boys gotta have a hobby," replied Rainey shrugging. "Maybe that will be our next date. How about you Tamara? Have you chosen any loser boyfriends over friends lately? I heard about your little brawl at the football game," she smiled shaking her head. "You're a real class act yourself. Inquiring minds want to know, during the brawl did you actually get a hair out of place or get a crease in whatever designer label you happen to be wearing that night. Sorry I missed the chance to see you rolling around in the grass like a commoner. You're parents must be so proud of their little princess."

"Has it all come down to this? So are we going to sit here and trade insults with each other all night?" asked Alicia staring from one to the other.

"Works for me," was Rainey's flippant reply. "Tamara threw down the gauntlet and I picked it up."

"I thought juvie's had curfews. Shouldn't you be home under house arrest or something? My bad," replied Tamara adding fuel to the fire. "Where's your ankle bracelet Rainey?"

"Give it a rest, both of you!" Alicia yelled trying to maintain her grip on sanity. Their arguing and prattle was the last thing she wanted to hear.

Silenced filled the tree house as each of the girls reflected on their first meeting. They met at a Sims Electronics picnic about ten years ago.

The three of them bonded instantly. They spent the afternoon playing games. That day three little girls bridged the gap between all racial and religious boundaries and formed a special friendship. They brought three families from totally different backgrounds and social standing together as an extended family.

Tamara's dad called them the trio of trouble. Where you found one, the others were usually not far behind.

Tamara's father, Thomas Sims was owner and CEO of Sims Electronics. Alicia's father, Miguel was an Account Executive and Rainey's mom, Shannon was an accountant for the Sims family business.

The trio's mothers made sure the girls got together often to play. Although they lived miles apart, they practically lived at each other's houses.

The girls wanted a special place they could call their own. Tamara's dad told them to draw up the plans and he would make it happen.

The girls excitedly drew up the blueprints. Thomas Sims hired a carpenter to build the girls own private sanctuary.

The tree house had ceilings high enough for an adult to stand up in and large enough to accommodate at least six people comfortably. It even had a small refrigerator, indoor bathroom, a sink, and electricity. It had all the comforts of home.

They added mats for the floor, a small television, radio, and throw pillows. The girls spent a lot of time at the tree house. There they were free to be themselves.

Their sanctuary was a place they came to think, talk and share their hopes and dreams for the future. No boys or adults were allowed.

The tree house was about 100 yards behind the Sims house. The girls begged and pleaded, but they were not allowed to spend the night there until they were older.

The first night they spent there was for Alicia's 12th birthday. After the birthday party at her house, her father brought them to the tree house to spend the night. It was a surprise and all the girls were screaming with excitement.

When they arrived at the tree house Janet Sims, Tamara's mom had already stocked the refrigerator with sodas, fruit, and chips. She decorated the tree house with streamers and balloons. There were sleeping bags and pillows for all the girls.

They stayed up most of the night munching and talking about boys. Not one of them had a boyfriend, but they each had crushes.

Through the years, they shared their innermost secrets with each other. They were not just friends, but sisters.

"Mr. Sims made the tree house for all of us," Rainey said breaking through the deadly silence. She looked around the tree house with affection. "This was our special place. Here we shared our hopes and dreams for the future. What happened to us? Where did it all begin to go wrong?"

"The Spanish tease tried to steal my boyfriend and you became easy Rainey, the girl who couldn't keep her legs together if her life depended on it."

"That's a lie and you know it," seethed Rainey. "But then you know all about liars Tamara. Nathan was a liar and so was Greg. I never slept with him. He spread the rumor to get back at me. Zeke was the first and only boy I had the misfortune to sleep with and I will regret the rest of my life."

"I didn't have to steal Nathan. He was never yours to begin with. It was all a game to him and you fell for it. You lost faith in a friend over a lie. He tested you and you failed miserably. And as for the name calling," Alicia hissed getting to her feet, "don't even go there." She and Tamara faced off. "Does your brain stop working properly when a boy walks by or what? You fell for Rodney's crap just as easy. Were you that naïve or just hard up? You threw away your virginity on a piece of trash that wasn't even worth it! You will be lucky if he didn't give you some disease! He's slept with half the sophomore class! I give you two snaps down." She snapped both fingers and placed her hands on her hips. "I thought you were more hip. You were pretty stupid for a sista," she finished snidely. Tamara moved closer. "Back off or bring it."

"I'll bring it all right, but can you handle it."

"Enough!" Rainey yelled getting uneasily to her feet. She stepped between the two angry girls. "Both of you need to back off. Look at us fighting over stupid boys. Boys who aren't even worth the argument we're having. We all made mistakes. No one is perfect. We all made bad choices and we have to live with the consequences of our actions."

Rainey's legs buckled beneath her. Alicia and Tamara caught her before she fell. Both girls were frowning as they eased her back down to the cushions.

"What's wrong with you Rainey?" Alicia asked eying her curiously. "What happened to you? You look pale. Are you sick?"

Rainey remained silent as tears dripped down her face and wet her white t-shirt. Cloaked in darkness, no one could see her cry.

"You're right Nathan wasn't worth fighting for. He certainly wasn't worth losing a friend over. I made a mistake with him. We were friends once," Tamara added. "We took a blood oath. What happened to that friendship? What happened to us? We let boys come between us."

"No you let boys come between us," snapped Alicia pointing at Tamara. "At least Barbie here didn't ditch us for boys. She ditched us for God only knows what."

"No, she ditched us to piss off her parents. She craves attention. It doesn't matter if it's good or bad attention as long as she gets their attention. How accurate am I Rainey?"

"You're both right," Rainey said softly pushing her long blonde hair behind her ears. "I did a lot of stupid things to get my father's attention. I pushed you guys away and I've lived to regret it. High School is a place where you need all the good friends you can get. I'm not talking about the phonies and fakes we've all been hanging around with. I'm talking about true friendship like we had."

"Had, being the key phrase," Alicia remarked softly. "Things change and people change and not always for the better. We are all proof of that. We all changed and we drifted apart. It happens to the best of friends. Why are we even discussing this? It's too late for us to rebuild now. The bond has been broken by each one of us. It's been a long day and I personally do not want to take a ride down memory lane. If you two want to leave, you can. I'm staying right here."

"I'm staying as well," Rainey seconded. "I'm not sure I can make it back down those stairs right now even if I tried."

"Are you high or something?" Tamara asked eying her suspiciously. "I hear Zeke's into a little bit of everything. Tell me you're smarter than that. Tell me you are not into drugs."

"No, I'm not high. I don't do drugs. I may be stupid, but not that stupid." She stopped talking and looked at Tamara and Alicia.

"But you obviously did something or you wouldn't be here." Tamara guessed. "Look Rainey, I know we all have our differences, but as long as we're inside this tree house. Everything we say to each other stays inside. That's the promise we made."

"I'm trusting the two of you to keep my secret. I want you both to swear on our past friendship what I say here tonight will go no further. You both have to swear. I need my friends right now. I need you guys. I don't have anywhere else to go or anyone else I can turn to. If my mom finds out what I've done, she'll send me to live with my dad. I'm all out of chances with her. I don't want to move to Florida. I want to stay here." Her voice cracked and the tears started flowing again.

Tamara put her battery operated lantern flash night in the middle of the circle. This illuminated all their faces.

Moving towards her, they all crossed their arms and held hands in the fashion of the secret oath they formed several years ago. As long as the circle remained unbroken, so would their friendship. All secrets revealed in the tree house would go no further. This was their secret pledge to one another.

"We are sisters. We are friends. We will stand together through thick and thin," they chorused gripping each other's hand.

"Tell us what happened and we promise it will go no further," Tamara said all traces of malice were gone.

Rainey's eyes met Alicia's and waited for a response from her. After a brief hesitation, Alicia nodded in agreement.

Chapter 2

Rainey's Story

Rainey Michaels came from a broken home. Her parents led separate lives long before her father ever walked out the door. Her parents divorced when she was ten years old.

Ken Michaels sued for joint custody and won. They had no idea how this would confuse and tear their daughters life apart.

Her father married a few months after the divorce was final. He and his new wife, Chloe moved two blocks away from Rainey and her mother.

As part of the custody agreement, she would spend two weeks with each parent until she reached the age of eighteen. This arrangement worked great for her parents, but it took its toll on her. She didn't know if she were coming or going half the time. Half her things were at her mom's house and the other half were at her father's.

Rainey's world of half and half came tumbling down around her, when her father was offered a job in sunny Florida. Her father and

Chloe moved to Florida and she stayed in Dallas with her mother.

He promised her he would see her every couple of months, on spring breaks and during the summer breaks. Of course, it didn't quite work out that way. They would make plans for her to fly out and something would always come up at the last minute.

A year after their move, Chloe had twin boys. Rainey spent her spring break and summer vacations in Florida. She loved her father and her little brothers. Even Chloe was growing on her. Her stepmother went out of her way to make her feel welcome.

Everyone seemed happy to see her when she came except for her father. He was always busy and couldn't seem to find time to spend with her. Chloe would try to make up for it, by doing things with her, but it wasn't the same. She needed her father.

As the years passed, she only went for summer vacation and her visits became shorter and shorter. This was her choice. She didn't want to be in Chloe's way.

Her father never took time off to spend with her. He left it up to Chloe and the kids to entertain her.

Rainey craved attention from her father. She would purposely do things to get into trouble, so her mother would call him. It seemed to Rainey the only time she talked to him was when she was in trouble. This quickly became an ongoing pattern. She was always in trouble and in and out of juvenile detention. She saw more of her parents when she was in trouble than she had in the past several years.

Shannon Michaels was the accountant for Sims Electronics. She was a workaholic and worked from sunup to sundown.

This left Rainey alone and unsupervised in the evenings. She unjustly earned a reputation of being fast and loose from a jock she refused to put out for. No one believed her innocence and she didn't care. It didn't help matters she hung out with the wrong crowd, smoking and drinking the afternoons away.

The trio of trouble was no more. Rainey pulled away from them when they started telling her how to live her life. Alicia preached at her constantly about right and wrong.

Tamara was always on her case about getting in trouble.

The big split came when Tamara's boyfriend kissed Alicia. Nathan was a pig. He convinced Tamara Alicia was after him and said she kissed him. Alicia forced Tamara to choose sides and she sided with the loser she thought was her boyfriend. Boy was she surprised a few weeks later when she caught him with another girl at a high school football game.

She heard through the grapevine Tamara was with Rodney now. Tamara was a magnet for losers. She went from bad to worse.

Alicia was still with the love of her life, Franco Morales. Franco was cute in a nerdy sort of way. He adored Alicia and vice versa.

She and Tamara were sitting in the cafeteria one day, when Alicia floated in on a cloud. She was smiling from ear to ear as she held out her hand.

"What is that?" asked Rainey touching the silver heart ring. Alicia and Tamara looked at each other and burst into laughter. "Care to share the joke?"

"It's a purity ring," smiled Alicia. "Franco and I had a ceremony and gave each other the rings. It signifies out faith in God and each other."

"Okay I'll break it down for you Rainey," laughed Tamara. "It means they agreed to wait until they are married to have sex."

"Oh! That's an adorable sentiment. I hope you guys make it that long." She took a bite of her apple. "My guess is you won't." Alicia made a face at her.

"Thanks Rainey are you speaking from experience now?" asked Alicia eying her warily. "You haven't done it, have you. I've heard the rumors, but I don't believe you would do something like that with Greg. He's such a dumb jock."

"No, Alicia, I'm still pure as the driven snow."

"Why do you make it sound like it's a bad thing?" Alicia persisted.

"I didn't say it was a bad thing."

"Okay enough with the virgin talk," Tamara stepped in. "Let me see your ring." She lifted Alicia's hand to inspect the ring. "It's beautiful. You're beaming."

"I hate to cut this short guys, but I'm in detention again," said Rainey getting up from the table. "I'll talk to you later."

She met her boyfriend Zeke in detention. That should have been her first clue he was bad news. Instead, it drew her to him. Zeke was like no one she ever met before.

The more her mother objected, the more she wanted to see him. She went behind her mother's back at every opportunity to see Zeke. She and her mother didn't agree on much lately.

The day she came home late from school, her mother came home early. When Rainey walked in the door, she froze when she saw her mother.

"Where have you been?" asked Shannon Michaels with crossed arms. Rainey said nothing as she came in the door. "Answer me Rainey. It's six o'clock. You should have been home hours ago."

"I was hanging out," she said evasively dropping her backpack on the sofa. "Something smells good. What's for dinner?"

"Don't you try and change the subject young lady! Where were you?"

"Practice ran late. It's no big deal mom. It's not even dark outside yet."

"It's a big deal when you lie to me. I know for a fact you are no longer on the cheerleading squad. They kicked you off because of your behavior. You want to try for the truth now. Were you with Zeke?"

"Yes, I was with Zeke."

"You're grounded for the next two weeks. I don't want you any where near that irresponsible walking train wreck. He's trouble Rainey and one day he will get you into more trouble than you can handle."

"I can take care of myself. I've been doing it for years. It's not like you and dad are around to help me out. He's in another state and you are always at work. Zeke is the only person I can depend on. He's there for me mom. You never are." Rainey ran from the room in tears. She thought that was the end of it, but her mother followed her.

"I'm tired of the acting out Rainey. You are skating on thin ice young lady. I spoke with your father tonight. He thinks you should come live with them for a while."

"What?" she asked in disbelief. "You're trying to get rid of me! Why should that surprise me? You never wanted me in the first place. I was an accident. Why would he want me there? He ignores me any time I'm around. Why don't I save you both the trouble and leave home? You're rid of me and so is he!"

"Is that what you think?" asked her mother angrily. "You think I don't want you. You think I don't love you. I bust my butt to give you the kind of life I never had. I make sure you have the best of everything and you appreciate nothing! The more I give the less you appreciate it. Do you think it's easy for me being a single parent? I have sacrificed my entire life for you and this is the thanks I get!"

"I never asked to be born! No one told you to trap dad by getting pregnant! That's right Mom. I overheard your argument the night he left. You deliberately got pregnant so he would marry you. You preach to me about doing the right thing, but I guess that rule doesn't apply to you. You should have had an abortion. I should never have been born! It's what dad wanted. He never wanted me. He gave you the money for an abortion so why didn't you get one. It would have solved all our problems."

Her mother staggered at the cruelty of her daughter's words. She stared at her daughter like she was seeing a complete stranger. Saying nothing in her own defense, her mother left the room.

Rainey sat down on the bed and cried. She didn't mean any of what she said to her mother. She was feeling neglected and lashing out.

Thirty minutes later, her mother came back with a large black garbage bag in her hand. She opened drawers and took out certain items.

"What are you doing mom? Those are my things."

"Since you obviously don't appreciate anything I do for you, why don't I just take all the brand names and give them to charity. I'm sure someone else would like them and appreciated them. You obviously don't." She yanked open the closet door and took out jeans and more shirts.

"Fine, take them. They are jus things." Her eyes grew round as saucers when her mom picked up the Harley Davidson jacket. "Mom, no," she pleaded. "Not the Harley jacket. Dad bought it for my birthday."

"But they are just things Rainey," she threw back at her. She stuffed the jacket in the bag. "I'm finished keeping you in Tommy's and whoever the latest trend is. Let's see how you like shopping at Wal-mart and Payless. If you need anything else, either call your dad or get a job. Babysitting pays about six bucks an hour. If you slip out the window, you are grounded for life." Shannon Michael's slammed the bedroom door behind her.

Rainey was livid when her mother left the room. She took all her favorite designer name outfits. She dropped down to the bed and let out a frustrated scream.

* * *

Rainey and Zeke quickly became an item. She let him talk her into all sorts of dumb stunts. One of her shining moments of stupidity was helping him steal beer from a convenience store. They almost got caught.

Smashed, Zeke dropped Rainey home. On his way home he hit a pole and totaled his father's pick-up truck. He walked away with only a broken arm. Zeke was lucky.

When Shannon's mother heard about the accident she threw a fit. She ordered Rainey to stay away from him.

Her mom was working late as usual, when Zeke brought her home after school. They were making out on the couch as usual.

They had oral sex on a regular basis, but they had never gone all the way. She always put the brakes on things before they went that far.

"I love you Rainey," said Zeke kissing her neck. "I want to show you how much." His mouth covered hers in a hungry kiss.

"You mean go all the way." Rainey pulled away from him. "I don't know if I'm ready. It's a big step Zeke. Alicia thinks I should save myself for marriage."

"Alicia's a prude. Don't listen to her. Listen to me. I'll show you how to have fun. Trust me," he said unbuttoning her blouse. "You're ready. It will be so good between us. Let me be the one to make you a woman." He released her and handed her another beer. "Have another beer while you think about it."

"I don't think I need another beer," she giggled. "I think you're trying to get me drunk so you can take advantage of me. Is that the plan?"

"I would never take advantage of you. You did say your mom is working late again, didn't you." She nodded sipping her beer. "Let's go to your room and get comfortable."

"Let's not and say we did," she teased moving out of his reach. "My mom says you're only after one thing."

"You're mom hates me. She would say anything to keep us apart. Don't let her keep us apart Rainey. We belong together. I want more than one thing from you. I want you heart, mind, and soul and yes your body as well."

Rainey was nervous, but after a few beers, she lost all her inhibitions. He pulled her to her feet and led her to her bedroom.

"I love you," said Zeke undressing her. "You are so beautiful. No one will ever love you the way I do."

Rainey's mind was a bit fuzzy as she tried to focus on what Zeke was saying and doing. She stumbled and he helped her onto the bed.

"I think I had a little too much to drink," she slurred as she laid spread eagle on the bed.

"I think you're right." He leaned over her and unfastened her jeans. "Let me put you to bed," he smiled wickedly. Wrapping her arms around his neck, she pulled his head down to hers and kissed him.

Rainey wasn't aware of much until she felt s sharp stabbing pain. She struggled against Zeke trying to push him away.

Nothing she heard or read had prepared her for this moment in her life. Her body felt like it was being ripped to shreds as they became one. There was a lot of grunting and heavy breathing on Zeke's part and then it was over.

Rainey lay frozen and stunned as he moved off of her. Her tears wet the pillow as she cried silent tears.

"Don't cry princess," crooned Zeke kissing away her tears. "It will be better next time. I promise."

"I'm never doing that again," she stated adamantly pulling away from him. She shuddered in revulsion at the thought of a doing it again. "It was awful and it hurt. Don't expect a repeat performance. I think you should leave."

"Let me at least regain my strength before you kick me out of bed." He lay down and went to sleep. Zeke was already snoring in the bed next to her.

Making love was not what she dreamed it would be. She would always regret giving her virginity to a 16 year-old boy who couldn't appreciate the gift. She waited 15 years for this moment and she was more than disappointed. She was disillusioned by the whole encounter.

Why do people do this? It's horrible and it's disgusting. I'm all sweaty and I feel dirty. Sex is a messy affair.

Rainey eased out of bed. Her whole body ached. She walked across the hall and took a shower. Sliding down to the floor under the running water, she cried.

Zeke was still there when she came out of the bathroom. He was dressed and sitting on the bed putting on his sneakers.

"Did you use protection?" she asked innocently. "I don't' remember if you used a condom or not."

"Don't worry about it. You're safe. You can't get pregnant the first time. Trust me," he said getting to his feet. "I'll give you a call later."

She watched him leave the room without a word. She didn't trust him. She wasn't even sure at this point, if she liked him.

After that day, her life changed forever. Zeke assured her she couldn't get pregnant the first time. Like everything else, he told her, she had foolishly believed him.

They had sex several times after that night, all of which Zeke did use a condom. Rainey didn't enjoy sex. She only did it to keep her boyfriend happy.

Afterwards, she felt dirty and used. She cried in the shower and swore never to do it again, but each time Zeke pressured her, she gave in.

Rainey thought nothing of her missed cycle. She swung her feet out of bed and a wave of nausea hit her. Scrambling for the bathroom, she threw up.

Her mom knocked on the door to make sure she was up. She told her mom she was sick and couldn't go to school.

"What's wrong?" asked her mother barging into the room. She put her hand on Rainey's forehead. "You're not running a fever. That's a good sign."

"It's cramps," Rainey lied curling into a fetal position. She wished to God it were cramps.

"I'll be right back," said her mother leaving the room.

When Shannon left the bedroom, Rainey bolted for the bathroom again. She wouldn't have believed there was anything left in her stomach to throw up. She quickly rinsed out her mouth and ran back to bed.

That was close.

She barely made it back to the bed, before her mother returned with the water and aspirin. Rainey took the pills and drank the water.

"Rest today and tomorrow you are back at school young lady. Get some rest. I have to get to the office." Her mother placed a warm kiss on her forehead.

She was too naïve to know what was wrong. She assumed it was something she ate the night before. After a few days, she figured out she was pregnant.

Rainey was horrified. She cried for three days straight. She was terrified to tell her mother. She couldn't bear to see the disappointment in her eyes. She had caused her mother so much pain already. This would be the final nail in her coffin.

Her mother threatened to send her to live with her father if she had one more screw up. This was more than a screw up. This was a complete disaster. She was fifteen and pregnant.

She hadn't seen Zeke for the past couple of days. She couldn't call Alicia or Tamara. She didn't want or need to hear a lecture about the consequences of premarital sex from Alicia. Not having anyone else to turn to, she called Zeke.

Rainey paced the room nervously waiting for him to get there. She wasn't going to beat around the bush. She was going to come straight out with it.

Zeke, I'm pregnant. Zeke, you're going to be a daddy. Zeke you lied to me. It is possible to get pregnant the first time you have sex. What are we going to do with a baby? My mom is going to kill me.

When the doorbell rang, she jumped. Wiping her sweaty palms on her jeans, she walked over and opened the door.

"Hi, come in." She stepped back for him to enter the house.

He came inside, pulled her into his arms, and kissed her. Rainey broke off the kiss and put some distance between them.

"What's wrong with you? Isn't this why you called me?" he asked sitting down on the sofa and patting the spot next to him.

"No, that's not why I called you. Is sex all you think about?" she snapped.

"Pretty much. I'm a teenage boy. What do you expect me to think about? Come sit by me?"

He patted the space beside him again. She walked over and sat down beside him on the sofa.

"Zeke, I'm pregnant."

"You're what?" he asked loudly. Zeke shot to his feet and moved away from her like pregnancy was something he could catch. He stared at her dumbfounded.

"I think you heard me the first time." She got up from the sofa and faced him. "I'm pregnant."

"Okay. So, what do you want me to do about it? Is it mine?" he asked shrugging his shoulders.

Rainey was appalled he could ask her such a question. She reacted instinctively by slapping. Furious, she marched over to the door and opened it.

"Get out of my house." He kicked the door shut with his foot. "How can you even ask me such a question? You are the only person I've been with! My mom was right about you. You are scum and you were only after one thing. I guess now you can walk out that door. You got what you wanted."

"Calm down. You're mom is not right. I care about you. Let's talk this through. We have some decisions to make."

"There is nothing to talk about," she said pushing her hair behind her ear. "I want you to leave. I will handle this on my own."

"No you can't. You need me."

"I need you like I need a hole in my head. Listening to you got me in this situation. Get out of my house."

"Fine Rainey. Have it your way. Call me when you calm do. We need to figure out what to do about this situation."

"This is not a situation," she snapped glaring at him. "This is a baby, our baby."

She slammed the door behind him. Walking over to the sofa, she dropped down to the sofa and gave in to her tears of misery.

She sat on the couch waiting for her mother to get home from work. All her choices were gone. She had to tell her mother the truth and suffer the consequences.

Rainey braced herself for the lecture and the disappointed look. She knew there would be tears from both of them. She also knew her mother would blame herself.

The ringing telephone interrupted her thoughts. She stared at the caller id with dread. It was her mother's office. She waited several seconds before picking it up.

"Hello," said the strangled voice.

"Honey, it's me," said Shannon. "I have to work late again sweetheart. I'll be there around ten." Rainey bit her lip and gripped the phone. She fought back the fresh onslaught of tears that threatened to fall. "Is something wrong? You sound funny."

"I think I'm coming down with a cold," Rainey sniffed thinking quick on her feet. "I'll take some medicine and get to bed early. I love you mom."

"I love you too sweetie. Are you sure you're okay?"

"I'm fine." Rainey bit her lip to keep from crying.

"Okay. I'll see you in the morning. Please eat something for dinner besides popcorn and lock up the house before you turn in."

"I will." Tears ran down her cheeks as she hung up the phone. Picking it up again, she dialed Zeke's number. "Can you come over? We need to talk."

They talked for what seemed like hours about their choices. They were too young to get married. She was a freshman in High School and Zeke was a sophomore.

In the end, Zeke convinced her it was best for everyone if she had an abortion. They both felt it was the only choice she could make.

He told her he would check around with some of his friends and find out whom other kids used for abortions. They agreed to get together tomorrow.

***

Zeke called her to say he would be picking her up from school the next day. He had some information to share with her about their situation.

Rainey got in the car without saying a word. She was still ticked off at him. If she had, any one to turn to right now, she never would have told him about the baby.

"I think you should have an abortion. We can't keep this baby. I'm only sixteen and you're fifteen. It would ruin our life."

"I can't have an abortion," she said shaking her head. "You want me to kill our baby. I can't do that."

"Technically it's not a baby, yet. Until the fetus is. . "

"Stop," said Rainey holding up her hand. "I don't even want to know how you know that. When was the last time you picked up a book about anything? Just how many girls have you knocked up and taken to a clinic?"

"I've asked around and I found a nurse who performs abortions all the time,' he said ignoring her question. " She'll do one for us for $250. I can get the money. I arranged for us to meet her at the clinic tomorrow night around 7:00 P.M."

"You've already made the arrangements without consulting me."

"What's there to consult? You can't have this, baby."

"This is wrong," she reasoned. "I should talk to my mother about this. This doesn't feel right."

"You're just scared. It's already a done deal. I made all the arrangements today. I'll pick you up tomorrow night. Just sneak out of the house the way you always do. You'll be home before your mom gets home from work. This is what's best for everyone Rainey. I'm not ready to be a parent and neither are you. We're just kids ourselves."

You're right," she said sadly shaking her head. "I can't see you as a father either. A child deserves better than us for parents."

They were both silent the rest of the way to her house. Rainey got out of the car, slammed the door, and went inside.

As she waited for 6:00, she prayed her mother would come home in time to stop her. She prayed someone would stop her.

Mom where are you when I need you? I need you right now. Please come home in the next fifteen minutes and save me from myself.

When the time came to leave, she didn't bother to sneak out her window. Her mother wasn't home so she walked out the front door.

Zeke assures her the nurse knows exactly what she's doing. She won't ask any questions and it'll only cost them $250. Rainey was afraid to ask where he got the money, but he told her he would pay for the abortion.

Rainey feels a sense of foreboding as she walks into the building. It's after hours and the clinic is in complete darkness.

A chill went down her spine as they follow the nurse to the back of the building. She turns on the lights and takes them to a room. The smell of anesthetic fills the air and almost chokes Rainey.

She listened as the nurse explained the D&C procedure. She would lie on her back with her feet in stirrups. The nurse would apply a shot of anesthetic to her cervix to numb her. She would use some type of seaweed to help dilate the cervix. If necessary, the cervical muscle will be stretched further with cone-shaped rods until the opening was wide enough to allow the abortion tools to pass into the uterus. The nurse would next use a loop-shaped knife to scrape the walls of her uterus. The knife would cut the baby and placenta into smaller parts to make it easier for her to pull them through the cervix.

Rainey's stomach recoiled at the description and she bolted from the room. She found the restroom just in time. Leaning over the toilet, she proceeded to empty the contents of her stomach, not once, but repeatedly.

Oh God, I can't do this. She gave me more information than I ever wanted or need to know. I can't let her do that to my baby. This is wrong. I've tried not to think about what happens during the procedure, but she made it real for me, too real.

Rainey sat on the toilet and locked the bathroom door. Within minutes, Zeke was knocking on the door.

"Rainey, are you okay? Please come out of the bathroom. Honey, I know it sounds awful, but we have to do it. We don't have a choice."

Rainey said nothing as she stared at the door. She rocked back and forth holding her hands across her stomach.

I want my mommy. I want my daddy. I can't do this. I am to young to have to make this kind of a decision.

"You have to get her out of there," said the perturbed nurse. "We only have about an hour before we have to be out of here. Regardless of what happens, you owe me $250. Time is money. If you can't get her out of there within the next five minutes, I'm leaving."

"You'll get your money," snapped Zeke. "Rainey, open the door. Think about it honey. Do you want to spend the rest of your life tied to me? What would we do? I guess we could move in with your mother or father. My parents would never take us in. I can just see Shannon and I sitting at the dinner table each night. I can get a job at McDonalds and maybe you can work at Burger King? Is this the kind of life you want?"

Rainey opened the door and walked out. There was no way she would be tied to this boy for the rest of her life.

She wasn't so sure this was the right thing, but she couldn't tell her mother she was pregnant either. Something deep inside her was urging her to walk away, but she pushed the feeling aside. This was her only way out. She had to go through with the abortion.

Rainey was numb as she lay on the cold white table with her feet in the stirrups. She was trying to imagine herself anyplace, but here.

She was told to scoot all the way down and it would be all over soon. She did as she was instructed and closed her eyes to block out the bright light beaming down on her.

Rainey tried to not think about what the nurse was doing to her body. She didn't want to think about the life she was ending. She wanted to concentrate on he future. She had her whole life ahead of her. Her baby would be gone, but she knew it would haunt her the rest of her life.

Rainey tensed as she felt the cold metal slide into her body. Tears slipped down her eyes to wet her hair. She bit her lip to keep from crying out.

This wasn't supposed to happen! I'm not supposed to be here! Where did my life go so wrong? If I live through this, I'm never having sex again!

She heard the nurse's voice telling her she would have to open her cervix. Rainey resisted the urge to close her legs. She explained to her she would feel a little pain and some pressure. The nurse told her to grip Zeke's hand if she needed too.

Rainey did as she was instructed grabbing Zeke's hand in a death grip. She saw him wince in pain and received a small amount of satisfaction from this.

Why do I have to feel all the pain and guilt? This was his baby too. I'm not going to think about it. I'm on a white sandy beach in Florida with my dad. We're playing in the water. The twins are also there. We're having a wonderful time. Oh daddy! Where are you when I need you? I need you now. I've always needed you, but you were never there.

After it was over, her whole body hurt. She wasn't sure if the pain was real or if it was all in her mind. Was this the beginning of her mental anguish?

Zeke helped her ease down from the table. The nurse told her to take it easy for a couple of days and then she would be back to normal.

Normal. What did that mean? There was nothing normal about what she did. Rainey doubted her life would ever be normal again.

Zeke paid the nurse and helped her into the car. On the drive home, no words were spoken by either of them. There was nothing to say. Tonight they killed everything between them.

Rainey lay on her bed hugging her teddy bear. She cried into her pillow wishing she could go to her mother for comfort. Looking around her pink frilly bedroom, she felt out of place. This beautifully decorated little girl's room was no longer hers. She didn't feel she had a right to be here. She felt dirty and used and she had to get out of there.

She winced as she pulled herself from the bed. With tears in her eyes, she packed her duffle bag. She wrote a letter to her mother explaining everything and saying goodbye. She left the letter by the coffee pot. The first thing her mother did each morning was turn on the coffee pot.

Giving the house one last look, she walked out the front door and locked the door behind her. She didn't belong here anymore either. She knew where she belonged. There was only one place she could go. She could always go to the tree house. She always felt safe there.

She rode the bus across town and then walked the rest of the way. Her heart was breaking as she stared up at the comforting shelter of the tree house. She felt weak and staggered almost losing her footing. She noticed the electrical fuse box, but decided against turning on the power.

Rainey didn't want to risk anyone seeing the light and coming out to investigate. Her plan was to stay in the tree house until she figured out where she was going. She had fifty dollars in her duffle bag along with a bottle of water, a sandwich and two packages of peanut butter crackers. She knew she couldn't get far with what she had, but she couldn't face her mother or father after what she did. She couldn't face herself.

Rainey finished her story and they all had tears pouring down their faces. Each had their own secret to tell and before the night was over, they would all share theirs.

Their hands were still clasped. Rainey's slackened and Tamara and Alicia refused to allow her to let go. Letting go meant giving up and none of them were ready to give up.

"Rainey, I'm so sorry about the baby," said Tamara. "You shouldn't have listened to Zeke. You should have gone to your mother and let her take you someplace. You don't even know if she used sterilized instruments. You could die of an infection or something. Zeke is an idiot and you went along with him. My God, Rainey, what were you thinking?"

"I can't tell my mother about this," said the croaked voice. "I have been nothing but a disappointment to my parents. Don't you understand? I did what my father wanted my mother to do about me." She bit her lip to keep from crying. "I killed my baby and in doing so, I killed a part of me. I took another person's life. How could I do that? What have I become?"

"Abortion is wrong. How could you do something like that? How could you kill an innocent baby? Didn't she explain to you what they do to the baby? It's inhuman. There are other options," Alicia lectured snatching her hand away. She got to her feet and faced her friends. "It was wrong Rainey. You killed an innocent baby! You should have talked to your mother about this or your priest or someone!"

"Alicia stop being so judgmental! This is not about you. It's about Rainey. She made a decision and she is the one who has to live with it. We know you are a good Catholic girl. We get that, but you don't have to shove it down our throats every chance you get. So back off and get off your soap box!"

"I am not on a soap box. I'm stating facts. An abortion cannot truly erase what has happened to her. Look at Rainey. Guilt is eating her alive. This is tearing her apart. Tamara you don't have to be Catholic to know what she did was wrong. Even a sometimes, good ole Southern Baptist like you can see this was wrong. There are always other options besides abortion. Would you have had an abortion in her position or would you have gone to your parents?"

"I don't know what I would have done Alicia," Tamara snapped. "This isn't about me or about you. I'll ask you the same question you asked me. Would you have had the baby? Could you in all honesty say you would have had this baby in her situation? I don't think so. You're Poppy would have a conniption, not to mention your Abuela would drop to her knees and say fifty hail Mary's and send you off to confession."

"Enough with the racial and religious slurs Tamara. When did you become a racist?" Tamara angrily crossed her arms over her chest. "This isn't a race issue. It's a matter of right and wrong. I killed my baby!" Rainey screamed. "I made the decision to end her life. I never gave her a chance. I could have carried my baby to term and given her up for adoption. Instead, I took the easy way out. It was selfish of me to have an abortion. I was only thinking about myself. I will never forget it and I will never forgive myself for what I've done. Alicia's right.

The guilt of what I did is eating at me. It's consuming me. It's suffocating me."

"I know you're hurting, but it's not the end of the world, at least not for you," Tamara reasoned. "We all have so much to live for. You can't let this tear you apart. You have to deal with the consequences of your decision. We all do. You will have other children. We are supposed to be young and foolish. We are also supposed to learn from our mistakes. Our mistakes are supposed to shape us into responsible adults. What if that's not the way our lives play out. Maybe we won't all be lucky enough to live to a ripe old age. Sometimes our mistakes haunt us the rest of our lives."

"Don't you guys find it strange we all ended up here at the same time," said Alicia turning to face them. "When was the last time any of us were here? We were all brought together for a reason. I'm still not sure what that reason is."

"Maybe we each have a story to tell. I've told mine. So which one of you is next? Tamara I think it's your turn. You're trying hard to tell us something. We're here to listen. Alicia will you rejoin the circle."

"I don't agree with what you did, but it doesn't stop me from caring about you and what happens to you." Alicia walked over to them and sat down. She caught the outstretched hands.

Chapter 3
Tamara's Story

Tamara Sims was the only child born to Thomas and Janet Sims until she was nine years old. It was a surprise to them all when Janet became pregnant after giving up on having another child.

Her world changed when Thomas James Sims II was born. Suddenly she wasn't the apple of her parent's eye anymore. Little T.J. was getting all the attention.

She resented her brother and wanted nothing to do with the little rug rat. Her mother would try to get her to hold him, but she always made some excuse to leave the room.

She didn't want to bond with him. She wanted him out of her house and away from her parents.

Tamara would escape from her little brother by going out to the tree house. There she wouldn't have to see, hear, or smell him. She would spend hours there playing with her

dolls and with her best friends Rainey and
Alicia.

Alicia and Rainey told her she should love
her little brother and be happy to have him.
They both had younger siblings they adored.
Tamara didn't think it was possible to love him
since he was getting all the attention.

Tamara's feeling changed the night her
little brother had to be rushed to the emergency
room. His temperature had spiked and the
doctor's were trying to get it down. It was
touch and go for several hours.

She cried, prayed, and begged God to give
her another chance with her little brother. She
promised to be the best big sister in the world
if he was spared.

T.J. recovered and Tamara kept her word.
She could still remember the first time she held
him in her arms. His tiny hand gripped her
finger, her heart melted, and a bond was
formed between them.

As the years passed her friends began to
blossom and she didn't. Alicia and Rainey both
got their cycle and were both wearing training
bras. She was still flat as a board with nothing
to train. While they were getting curves, she

was still tall and skinny. She was as thin and straight as a pencil. She prayed every night for breasts.

The summer before eighth grade, she started her period. Tamara was in Heaven although everyone else around her walked on eggshells at her mood swings. Her figure also filled out. She went from a training bra to a 34-C almost overnight. Hers hips rounded into the perfect hourglass figure.

The first day of school the boys did a double take as she walked by twisting a little more than was necessary. Tamara loved all the attention she was getting with her new and improved figure. She smiled and flirted as she made her way to her locker.

Her breasts were bigger than both Rainey and Alicia. She wore her uniform shirt a little too tight to accentuate her bust line.

Tamara got mad at Alicia for telling her she needed to tone down the make-up and buy a larger size blouse. She told her she was just jealous and didn't know anything about make-up or fashion.

The trio had other interests and didn't spend as much time with each other as they usually did. Tamara was on the drill team. Alicia was in Choir and Rainey was a cheerleader.

Their schedules didn't leave a lot of time for them to get together. Sometimes they ate lunch together in the cafeteria, but it was rare.

The summer before ninth grade, Tamara spent the summer in New York with her aunt Liz. Her aunt was an Advertising Executive who lived in Manhattan. Tamara had a wonderful time. They went to plays, concerts and just hung out together. She was not ready to go back home when the time came.

She came home about two weeks before school started and called Alicia and Rainey. Tamara excitedly told Alicia about her trip to New York.

Alicia was equally excited Franco had moved three blocks from her house. They tried to call Rainey for a three-way, but she wasn't home. They talked for a couple of hours before hanging up.

The first day of school, Tamara was a nervous wreck. She changed clothes five times and still didn't like what she was wearing.

Satisfied at last with her appearance, she jogged down the stairs.

"What do you think you are wearing?" asked Janet Sims eying her daughter with distaste. "You are not leaving this house looking like a happy hooker. Go change." She pointed towards the stairs.

"Mom, it's just a uniform," Tamara whined smoothing down her short skirt.

"A size bigger and it would still be a uniform. It is too tight, to short and too seductive. Tamara you're only fifteen."

"I'll be sixteen in three months. I like my outfit. It shows off my figure."

"I don't want you to show off your figure. Honey there are weirdo's out there who prey on young girls trying to dress and look older. I don't want there to be any question in anyone's mind about how old you are. You are fifteen. I expect you to dress like it and act like it. You are not leaving the house dressed like this. Find something else to wear or I will find something for you and believe me you won't like my choice." Tamara turned and went back up the stairs. "If you slam that door you're grounded for a week!" yelled her mother reading her mind.

Her parents were so old fashioned it was driving her crazy. They were still treating her like she was twelve. They were ruining her social life.

Tamara changed, but on impulse put the top and skirt into her backpack. What her mom didn't know wouldn't hurt her. She also dropped in her make-up case.

This went against another of the Sims house rules. She was so tired of all their rules. She felt like she was in prison. She was not allowed to wear make-up until she was sixteen. Tamara would be sixteen in three months so she didn't see what the big deal was.

Her mom dropped her about fifteen minutes early, which gave her enough time to slip into the bathroom and change back into the outfit she wanted.

She quickly made up her face and applied the plum lipstick to her heart shaped lips. Her light brown complexion was smooth, so no base was needed. She added blush, eye shadow, and eyeliner. She didn't add mascara because it wasn't as easy to take off. She smiled at the finished result.

Tamara saw Alicia in the hall and they embraced warmly. Alicia told Tamara because of Rainey getting into so much trouble the school put her on probation as a stipulation for her return.

About two months later, Tamara walked up on her boyfriend Nathan and Alicia having a heated argument. They both played it down and Alicia walked away calling Nathan a jerk.

A week later, she walked upon them kissing. If she hadn't seen it with her own eyes, she still wouldn't have believed it. Alicia always acted like she couldn't stand Nathan. It was all a lie to throw her off guard.

She shoved Nathan away and slaps him when she saw Tamara standing there. Tamara stared from one to the other waiting for someone to explain to her what she just witnessed.

"I always knew you were a creep," hissed Alicia wiping the kiss from her mouth with the back of her hand.

"Tamara, tell your friend to keep her hands and lips to herself," said Nathan feigning outrage.

"What? You've got to be kidding me. Nathan if you were the last creep on earth I wouldn't touch you." She turned angry eyes to her friend. "Please tell me you are smart enough not to buy into the game he's playing."

"She was all over me. You saw it with your own eyes, baby. She's jealous of you. She kissed me."

"You are a liar. She saw what you wanted her to see. Tamara is too good for you. She deserves better."

"What's going on?" asked Franco walking up. He looked from Alicia to Tamara for an answer to his question. He ignored Nathan altogether.

"This jerk kissed me."

"You kissed Alicia," hissed Franco grabbing Nathan by the front of his shirt and slamming him against the locker. "Do you have a death wish today playboy? I warned you once before to stay clear of my girlfriend. Three strikes and you're out."

"Stop it, all of you! Franco let him go."
Franco shoved Nathan aside. "This is not
Nathan's fault. Alicia how could you do this to
me? You are supposed to be my friend."

"I am your friend and I am insulted you
would believe him. Have I ever lied to you
about anything?"

"There's always a first time. You can't
stand the fact I'm happy or that Nathan wants
me and not you."

"He wants you," she repeated laughing.
"Like he's wanted half the Junior Class.
Tamara wake up. He's using you. Are you that
blind or just stupid?"

Tamara charged and Franco stepped
between the two girls. He wasn't going to let
them come to blows over a jerk like Nathan.

"Tamara, use your head and not other parts
of your anatomy. There is no way Alicia would
kiss Nathan. She despises him. He came onto
her a few weeks ago in the cafeteria."

"That's what you keep telling yourself
Franco and maybe you'll start to believe it.
Maybe she's tired of you professor."

"Even if she were, I doubt she'd come
looking for you in Special Ed. Come near

Alicia again I will personally rip your head off." He turned his attention back to Tamara. "Who are you going to believe Tamara, this lying creep or your best friend?"

"Come on baby. You don't need them. You have me now. Maybe it's time you made some new friends." He put his arm around her and started to lead her away.

"Don't do it Tamara," warned Alicia. "If you walk away with him, our friendship is over. I mean it. There will be no turning back."

Tamara hated being pinned in a corner, so she came out swinging. She did not do well with ultimatums. She didn't look back as she let Nathan lead her down the hallway.

When she got home, she dialed Rainey's number. She paced her bedroom with the portable phone waiting for Rainey to pick up.

She's probably out with that loser Zeke. I have no idea what she sees in him. He's nothing but trouble.

"Hello," said the friendly voice on the other end of the line. "I was just thinking about giving you a call."

"You are not going to believe what happened today. Alicia stabbed me in the back. She kissed Nathan."

"That was a joke, right," said Rainey bubbling over with laughter. "Alicia and Nathan, get real. You know she's head over hills in love with geek boy Franco."

"I'm telling you the truth," said Tamara angrily. "I saw it with my own eyes. She was kissing Nathan."

"Then you need glasses. Alicia loves Franco. You are her best friend. There is no way she would go after your guy. Maybe he kissed her."

"She called you didn't she," Tamara guessed. "She got to you first and as usual you are taking her side. You weren't there Rainey. I was. I know what I saw."

"Tamara grow-up. You saw what Nathan wanted you to see. The stage was set and you walked right into a show. He set you up. Face it, admit it, and move on. He's not worth this."

"Thanks Rainey. You have all the answers for my life, but yours is falling apart. Speaking of losers, where's that loser boyfriend of yours. Is he in juvie this week?"

"This is not about Zeke. This is about you and Alicia. We have been friends a long time for you to let this creep come between you."

"Nathan is not a creep," she denied hotly. "He's my boyfriend and I love him. I have no reason not to trust him."

"And you have a reason not to trust Alicia. Alicia is the most honest person I know. She doesn't lie. You were wrong and you know it. You owe her an apology."

"I don't owe her anything!"

"You are a spoiled brat. You can't even see the forest for the trees, but I'm sure eventually you will. When you realize what a jerk Nathan is, I hope it's not to late. Get over yourself," snapped Rainey slamming the phone down in her ear.

Tamara stared at the telephone in her hand. She angrily slammed down her phone as well. She didn't need Rainey or Alicia. She lost two friends that day.

Shortly after the incident with Alicia, Tamara discovered for herself what a jerk Nathan was. She caught him kissing another girl at a football game. She exploded and threw her soda in the girls face and punched Nathan in the eye. Nathan retaliated by slapping her. A boy who liked Tamara saw the incident and jumped on Nathan.

The girl who kissed Nathan jumped on Tamara. A brawl ensued and Security had to break it up. They were all escorted from the football stadium.

Tamara lied to her parents about what happened and told them a girl jumped on her because her boyfriend was looking at her. She couldn't tell them she lost her two best friends over a worthless teenage boy's lies.

Tamara felt like a complete idiot. Everyone was right about Nathan and she was wrong. The boy she loved had wrecked her life and betrayed her. Her heart was broken and there was no one she could confide in. They had all warned her it would happen and now she was alone.

Her pride wouldn't let her apologize to Alicia or Rainey. She doubted they would accept her apology after the horrible things she said to them.

After drill team practice, she sat on the steps waiting for her mother. She looked up in surprise when Rodney Carter sat down next to her on the step. Her heartbeat quickened.

Rodney was one of the most popular boys in school. He was also a junior and played first string on the football team.

"You're Tamara, right." She nodded not trusting her voice to speak. "Do you need a ride home? I could give you a lift."

"Yes, I'm Tamara. Thanks for the offer, but my mom's picking me up." She held out her hand to him. "It's nice to meet you Rodney. I've seen you around."

"I've noticed you as well. How could I not notice a beautiful fine young woman like yourself?" Tamara gushed at his compliment. "Would you like to go out sometime?"

"I'm not allowed to date yet," she confessed twisting her hands nervously in her lap. "I'll be sixteen in three months if you're willing to wait."

"I've already waited a lifetime for you," he smiled showing off perfect white teeth and dimples. He brings her hands to his lips.

Tamara thought she would faint. She could not believe she was sitting here with Rodney Carter and he was kissing her hand.

"Flattery will get you no where," she smiled removing her hand from his.

He reached out and brushed a strand of hair from her fair. Their eyes held as they stared at each other.

"Are you sure you don't need a lift home?" he asked looking down at the thin gold wristwatch on his arm.

"No. My mom would kill me if she drove all the way here to pick me up and I was gone. You could stay and meet her."

"Whoa," he said holding up his hands in defense. "I'm not really into the parent thing. I'll see you around Tamara."

Rodney left right before her mother showed up. She was still beaming as she watched him get into his black mustang convertible and peel out of the parking lot.

The next day at lunch, he came over and ate with her. Tamara felt like all eyes were on them.

"I think you're pretty terrific," smiled Rodney taking her hand in his. "I want you to be my girlfriend."

She was overjoyed, but paused when she saw Nathan coming their way. Their eyes locked as he passed by the table.

"I'd love to be your girl friend," said Tamara tearing her eyes from Nathan's retreating back. She pasted on a smile for Rodney.

Tamara was still smiling when he left the table. She looked up when some one stopped in front of her causing a shadow to cast over her.

"Tamara you're going from bad to worse. Rodney makes Nathan look like a choirboy. Just be careful. People aren't always what they seem."

"Alicia it almost sounds like you care, but I know that can't be it. We're not friends anymore. Why are you always trying to burst my bubble? Why can't you let me be happy? Why do you have to spoil everything?"

"Why can't you see what's right in front of you? Why do you keep picking these losers? You deserve better. Stop settling for second best."

"Why can't you mind your own business and butt out of mine? I didn't ask for your two cents nor do I want it. Have a nice lunch," seethed Tamara leaving the table.

Alicia was always trying to bring her down and burst her bubble of happiness. Who needed friends like her any way? She blew off the warning the same way she blew off the warning about Nathan. Rodney wasn't Nathan. He was a nice guy. Everyone liked him.

"Hey Tamara," said Nathan sitting down at her table. "Can I talk to you for a minute?"

She threw the napkin down on the table. Her appetite was gone and her day was going from bad to worse.

"What do you want Nathan?" She got to her feet. "Forget I even asked. I don't want to know. Feel free to sit down. I'm leaving."

"Tamara you're a nice girl, too nice for me and certainly too nice for Rodney. You're in way over your head with him. Don't do anything stupid rebounding from what I did to you."

"You mean because you cheated on me and made a fool out of me in front of the school. Then there was that small insignificant little thing like making me lose my best friend. Compared to what you've done to me, I think anything Rodney does is child's play. Have a nice lunch."

***

Over the next few months, she and Rodney were together all the time. She was on cloud nine when he gave her a gold heart and diamond promise ring.

She and Rodney would often sit out in his car after drill team and football practice. They would kiss and do a little petting, but nothing more.

This changed a few weeks later when Rodney started pressuring her to go further. He wanted to touch her below the waist. Tamara was hesitant at first, but he talked her into it.

"I went home sick today. Why don't you skip drill team and come with me? It'll be fun. I promise."

"My Mom would kill me if I left the campus. I would be grounded for life. I guess what she doesn't know want hurt me. So what do you have in mind?"

"Hop in and find out." Smiling she got into the car. She had no idea where they were going, but she got into the car with him. He took them to his parent's house. His parents

were at work so they were home alone. They
sat on the couch kissing and petting.

"Take off your panties," Rodney suggested
kissing her neck. "I want to touch you, nothing
more."

"I can't. I'm a virgin and I'm not ready to
go any further than we already have."

"So am I sweetheart. Despite the nasty
rumors about me, I'm still a virgin. I date a lot,
but I've never made love before. I've waited
my whole life for you. We can fool around
without actually having sex the old fashioned
way. I'll show you. Trust me. We'll both still
be virgins when we leave this room. I
promise."

Rodney went on to explain to her they were
not going to have sex the old fashioned way.
He promised her they would both still be
virgins when they left the house. He explained
to her what oral sex was.

Tamara was disgusted by the whole idea.
She could not imagine doing the things, he
wanted to do to her, or doing the things, he
wanted her to do to him.

While hesitant, she went along with him.
He was after all her boyfriend and she didn't

want to lose him. She knew if she didn't do them, some other girl would.

She missed practice twice the following week and went home with Rodney. They were both naked in his bed, when he first started pressuring her to go farther.

"I want to make love to you. I'm trying to be strong, but I want you so badly. We're practically lovers anyway, so why not take the next step. I want you so much it's killing me." He drowned out her protest with a kiss.

I can't," said Tamara breathlessly pulling her mouth from his. "I'm not ready to go all the way."

"Please baby," he begged pinning her arms to the bed above her head. "I love you." He planted kisses along her neck and collarbone. "We're promised to each other. You wear my ring. Honey everyone is doing it. Tell me you want it too." He pressed her down onto the sofa.

Tamara struggled for freedom in his embrace. He released her and she got quickly out of bed. She dressed and rushed from the room.

"Please take me back to the school. I think we should take a break from each other for a while. Things are moving way too fast for me. I need some time to think."

"I promise you I will only go as far as you let me."

That's what I'm afraid of.

***

The next week, she refused to go with him. She asked Rodney to back off and he did, but she hadn't meant all the way off. True she needed time to think, but she didn't think he would go away completely. She had not seen or talked to him in over a week.

Tamara knew she was in way over her head and needed someone to talk to. She couldn't talk to Alicia or Rainey because they weren't friends any more.

She was sure Alicia would read her the riot act about abstinence and waiting until marriage. She should have felt comfortable talking to her mother about the situation. Her mother was a volunteer counselor at a teen center and her own daughter was too afraid to confide in her.

She logged into a teen chat group on the Internet. Lurking in the background, she listened to the discussions. The debate went on for hours about whether or not to have sex before marriage. Some, where strongly opposed while others thought it was no big deal. When she logged off, she was no closer to finding the answer she was seeking.

Tamara didn't know what was the big deal any way. How many people actually waited until they were married in this day and age? Her parents did, but that was back in the old days. The Bible says its wrong, but that was also written back in the prehistoric days.

After wrestling with her conscious all night, she made the decision to wait. She knew she wasn't ready yet and Rodney would just have to understand and accept her decision. She prayed he would and not break up with her.

Her common sense fled the next day when she saw a girl cozying up to Rodney by his locker. They were flirting openly with each other. When she slipped him her phone number, Tamara knew she had to make a move or risk losing him. Drastic times called for drastic measures. She wouldn't be the first fifteen year-old girls to lose her virginity.

"Rodney, hi," said Tamara wringing her hands nervously. "I've been looking for you. You didn't return any of my calls. Are you trying to tell me something?"

"Excuse us Bridget," he said to the girl who was eying them curiously. "I might be able to catch up to you later." Rodney and Tamara both watched her walk away. "I've been around. I guess you weren't looking in the right places." He took his books out of the locker. "You asked for space and I've given it to you." He closed the locker and turned to face her. "I don't want you to feel pressured to sleep with me. Just know if you don't, someone else will."

"And that's not pressure. Is that a threat?" she asked crossing her arms over her chest. "If I don't put out you'll find someone else who will."

"No, Tamara that is reality. There are girls lined up to be with me and I chose you. You are the one wearing my promise ring, not them. I love you, but I'm not going to wait forever.

When you decide you're ready to grow up, call me."

"I'll meet you this afternoon," said Tamara. The words were out of her mouth before she knew it and it was too late to take them back.

"I'll see you after school." He leaned in and gave her a quick kiss on the lips. "I promise you won't regret your decision."

Tamara had all day to stew on her impulsive decision. When 2:30 p.m. came, she was a nervous wreck. She wanted to back out, but she didn't know how. She didn't want him to think she was a tease.

When they got to Rodney's house, they went straight to his bedroom. He kissed her and started undressing her. Tamara froze in his arms. He told her to relax and he stopped undressing her and pulled his shirt over his head.

Tears formed in her eyes and she wanted to leave. He kissed away her tears and told her he loved her. Rodney promised her it would be okay and he would never do anything to hurt her.

She trusted him and she believed him as he led her over to the bed. This is wrong her conscious told her, but she ignored it.

"Relax sweetheart. I won't hurt you. Trust me. You are so beautiful." He kissed her quivering bottom lip. "You are the girl I want to spend the rest of my life with. We were meant to be together."

"I'm not ready," said Tamara covering herself with her arms. "I thought I was, but I'm not. I'm sorry to disappoint you. I can't go through with this."

"Yes you can baby. I know you're not a tease. I need you. You can't just build up my expectations and let me down now. I love you. If you love me, prove it. Let me make love to you. You won't regret it. I promise. It's now or never."

Tamara believed all his lies. After a few minutes of excruciating pain, it was over. She lay there too stunned to move.

Where was the pleasure she read about in Romance books? She only felt pain and gladness when it was over. This is not how it was supposed to be. She was supposed to enjoy it too, wasn't she? In the movies, the couples were both happy and smiling afterwards. She didn't feel like smiling. She felt like crying. She was supposed to feel something other than regret at losing her virginity.

As Rodney moved away from her, she felt wetness on her leg. Her eyes flew to his in horror. The condom had ripped.

"Oh God" she screamed shoving him aside. She vaulted out of bed and ran to the bathroom. She quickly used it thinking this would expel any contents from her body. She washed the blood from her sore thighs before coming back into the room with a towel wrapped around her.

Tamara dressed quickly not looking at him. She couldn't face him after what happened. She feared she would get pregnant.

"It's okay. Calm down. You act like it's the end of the world. Nothing is going to happen. Besides, I have a low sperm count. You won't get pregnant the first time."

"It would be the end of the world as I know it. I'm not an idiot so don't talk to me like I am one. I know you can get pregnant the first time you have sex."

Nothing he could say would erase her fears. In one month, they would both know if their reckless afternoon produced a child neither of them was ready for.

A few weeks later, Tamara was relieved to get her cycle. She promised God she would never do anything like that again. She would wait until she was married.

Thinking about what could have happened, sent chills down her spine. She couldn't imagine telling her parents she was pregnant. She couldn't fathom rocking her baby in her arms.

When she got to school, she went looking for Rodney to tell him the good news. She knew he would be as revealed as she was.

She stopped in her tracks when overheard him and a girl arguing. Cindy was a senior and had a reputation for being a tramp.

"My partner before you tested positive for HIV. If I were you, I'd get out my little black book and start making some phone calls. If you'll recall our tryst about a month ago, we didn't use any protection."

"You've got to be kidding me." He hits the locker beside her head. "You skanky tramp, if you gave me AIDS, I will kill you," he hissed glaring down at her.

"You're the one who was so hot for me you couldn't wait. I guess that's what happened since your little girlfriend turned you down that day."

Tamara did something she had never done before in her life. She fainted. When she came to, she was in the nurse's office lying on a bed.

The nurse told her she called her mother and she was on her way to the school. She also told her Rodney was waiting outside to see her.

Tamara shivered as the conversation between Rodney and Cindy came back to haunt her. She didn't want to see or talk to him ever again.

She could have AIDS because of him. He was sleeping with other girls while sleeping with her. She felt used and very stupid for believing his lies.

When the nurse let him in, she told him she was fine. She also told him she never wanted to see him again. He left saying how sorry he was.

She ran into her mother's arms and cried. Not knowing what was wrong, her mother took her to the doctor for a check-up.

In the doctor's office with her mother outside waiting, she told the doctor she needed to be tested for AIDS.

She begged him not to say anything to her mother about the blood work. He told her he wouldn't say anything because it was routine to draw blood in situations like this.

.

"Tamara, have a seat," said her mom waving towards the sofa. "We need to talk." Tamara sat down next to her on the sofa. "I know we haven't talked in a while, but I think we need to. Are you pregnant?"

"No, Mom." She looked down at her hands and almost lost it. "I'm not pregnant."

"But you have been sexually active." The color seeping into her daughter's face gave her the answer she didn't want to hear. "Tamara you're fifteen years old. What are you thinking? You are ruining your life."

"How would you know? You never have time for me. You are either with T.J. or at the Teen Center. Where do I fit in? Should I make an appointment?"

"Don't you dare try to turn this around on me! I'm not the one who's fifteen and having sex. If you make a mistake, stand up and admit it. You are a Sims. We do not run from our problems or blame them on other people. Something is going on with you. When you're ready to talk, I'm here to listen."

I love you Mom.

After dinner, Tamara slipped out of the house. With her flashlight lantern, she made her way to the tree house.

"Go ahead and call me an idiot Alicia," Tamara said wiping the tears from her face. "You warned me about Nathan and you warned me about Rodney."

"I don't think you're an idiot and I would never say I told you say. You were taken in by two cons. Nathan is a jerk and Rodney has bedded half the school. He was a smooth talker. He probably did and said all the right things to reel you in."

"I second that," said Rainey squeezing her hand. "Okay so we are both idiots. Alicia is the only sane one in this group. She and Franco made the decision to wait. They still wear their purity rings to show the world their commitment to God and to each other. I have to admit before I thought it was pretty lame.

Now, I respect your decision to wait. I admire you for sticking with your beliefs" Rainey squeezed her hand. She looked at Alicia's finger and noticed her ring was gone. "Where's your ring?" Alicia lowered her head. "Not you too. I thought you and Franco agreed to wait. What happened? Okay, I don't mean what happened. I know what happened, but what changed your mind?"

"You and Franco did it?" Tamara asked. "Was it as disappointing for you as it was for me with Rodney? I don't know what I was expecting, but it sure wasn't wham bam thank you ma'am. Please tell us you did use protection. If you get pregnant, your father will be heartbroken."

"We can't always control our own destiny," snapped Alicia trying to pull away. Rainey and Tamara refused to let her hand go. Silent tears spilled down her bruised cheek as she dropped her head to her chest. "Sometimes we can't rebound from our mistakes. Sometimes the choices we make come back to bite us. Sometimes we put ourselves into stupid positions we can't always control. What can we do then? How do we rebound from something we had no control over to begin with? You both had control over what you did. You had a choice. I didn't! I had no choice!"

They both stared at her in confusion. Neither Tamara nor Rainey had any idea what she was talking about.

"When did this go from Tamara's problem to your problem? What are you trying so hard not to tell us? What happened to you Alicia? You've been trying to hide you face from us all night. We're not blind. We see the bruise on your cheek. Someone hit you. Who was it? I know it wasn't your father. He worships you. You're little speech about not controlling our own destiny tells us nothing traumatic happened to you?"

"Alicia, tell us," Tamara encouraged. "Who hit you? Tell us it wasn't Franco who did this. Is he a beating you?"

Alicia shook her head not trusting her voice to speak.

"We're not going anywhere Alicia," Rainey said softly. "You might as well tell us your story. It can't be any worse than ours. We are both Queens of Stupid. You are not. You are more level headed than we ever hoped to be. So who hurt you and why?"

Alicia removed the cap from her head. Her long dark hair tumbled down her back. Turning on her flashlight, she let it light up her face. Her friends both gasped at the bruise covering her check. Ignoring their stares, she raised her t-shirt to reveal several more bruises. Her throat had the perfect imprint from a hand. No part of her body was left unscathed.

She eased back down and caught their hands. She closed her eyes as flashes of earlier today hit her full force. She trembled in fear, Tamara, and Rainey's grip tightened on her hands. They waited patiently for her to tell them what happened.

"I love Franco and he loves me," she cried. "He would never hurt me. He doesn't even know about this. My father doesn't know about this. It's going to kill both of them when they find out what happened. This is going to ruin a lot of lives. Franco and I were waiting to be together, but we changed our mind. We decided we were ready to make love. Only that's not how the story goes. Franco didn't do this to me, his brother Hector did. He raped me and I can never face Franco again. It's my fault. I shouldn't have been there. I knew it was wrong. I wasn't ready. God, I wish I had waited! I should have trusted my instincts and gone home." Her voice faded and she was transported back in time.

Chapter 4

Alicia's Story

Alicia Perez was raised in a loving and happy home. Her father, Miguel worked as an Account Executive for Sims Electronics. He made enough money that after Alicia's brother Luis was born her mother quit her job to stay home with the children.

The Perez family enjoyed family outings and 10:30 A.M. Mass every Sunday. Afterwards, they would go out to lunch. It became a family tradition.

At the age of seven, she gave first confession and had her first communion. She wore a white lace gown her mother made. Alicia looked like a fairy princess in the dress. They had a special celebration dinner at the house with all the family afterwards. Her parents gave her a beautiful gold cross. Alicia vowed never to take it off.

Her ideal life fell apart when she was eleven. Alicia's mother was killed in an automobile accident. The death shook not only the foundation of her family, but her faith as well. She was angry with God and the world for taking her mother away. Through months of prayer and therapy, she was able to at least deal with her loss.

Her father was inconsolable. He pushed everyone away, including his children. Miguel Perez sent Alicia and her little brother, Joseph to live with his brother and sister-in-law for a year.

Alicia hated New Mexico and wanted to go home. She missed her father and her best friends Tamara and Rainey. They talked on the phone and wrote letters, but it wasn't the same.

She was overjoyed when her father came to get them. Rainey and Tamara had a welcome home party for her at the tree house. The trio of terror was together again.

As Alicia's body began to change, she had a hard time expressing her problems to her father. She was embarrassed to talk to him. Tamara's mother was a surrogate Mother to her. She took Alicia under her wing and explained the changes in her body.

Mrs. Sims also called Miguel to make him aware of what was going on with his daughter.

A bit embarrassed himself he agreed to let Janet handle the situation.

Alicia cringed when she thought back to the first time her father took her to buy sanitary napkins. Of course, she would pick up a box with no price tag. Her humiliation intensified when the checker called for a price check over the loud speaker. Completely mortified, she willed the floor to open up and swallow her.

She was equally embarrassed when he took her to get her first training bra. They were at the mall and her father handed her cash and waited outside while she went in to get it. Alicia had no idea what she needed. She was grateful when the sales girl took pity on her and helped her out.

Shortly after that, her Abuela/Grandmother came from Mexico to live with them. She never knew her grandfather. He died before she was born. Her Abuela spoke only broken English and only conversed with them in Spanish.

Under her guidance, Alicia learned everything she didn't already know about the Catholic faith. Abuela had them all going not only to Mass on Sunday, but prayer on Wednesdays and confession each week.

Through seventh grade, Alicia went to a private Catholic school. Her father was reluctant to send her to non-Catholic school, until Mrs. Sims stepped in and told him about Tamara's private school. He agreed to give it a shot and Alicia was overjoyed.

At thirteen going on fourteen, she felt like it was her first touch of freedom. Mrs. Sims arranged for her to be in the same room with Tamara.

Alicia met Franco Morales the first day of school. It wasn't exactly love at first sight for either of them. They were both used to being top student in their classes. She had finally met her academic match.

Franco looked so smart with his short black hair and small wire rimmed gold glasses. He was easily the most handsome boy she'd ever met.

Over the next several months, they challenged each other at every academic level. Their friendship was gradual.

"So Alicia are you and Franco still playing whose top dog in class? Who's winning this week?" Tamara asked taking a bite of her apple.

"Franco and I aren't playing anything," Alicia denied. "I admit he's my academic challenge. He is so cute."

"In a geekie sort of way," smiled Rainey. Alicia threw her napkin at her.

"I can see it now a match made in Academic Heaven," crooned Tamara placing her hands in a prayer pose and leaning them against her cheek.

"More like a match in Geek land," Rainey teased blowing Alicia a kiss. "I think Alicia is in love."

"Thanks guys. Just what I needed to hear. I knew I could count on my friends not to tease me unmercifully."

"Don't look now, but here comes your prince charming," said Rainey. Panic was etched on Alicia's face. "Breathe and relax. He's almost here."

"Is this seat taken?" asked Franco smiling at Alicia. She was so choked up no words came out. She shook her head no and he sat down next to her. Alicia's smile was so brilliant it lit up the cafeteria.

"Gotta go," said Rainey getting to her feet. "Tamara why don't you come with me?" Both girls were smiling as they left the table.

She found out through the rumor mill, Franco was at Hockadell through an Academic Scholarship. He lived on the south side of town.

As her friendship with Franco blossomed, her friendship with Tamara and Rainey deteriorated. Tamara was head over hills in love with a playboy and Rainey was hanging out with an older wilder crowd. She was smoking, drinking, and running wild.

Alicia and Franco had their first fight about her friends. He warned her they were both in over their heads with the new friends they chose.

She is eating alone in the cafeteria when Tamara's boyfriend sits down across from her. Alicia can't stand him and he knows it. She was not in the mood to make small talk with him.

"So is it true what they say about Spanish girls?" Nathan asked licking his lips as he gave her the once over.

"Since I don't know who they are and what they say, I can't answer your question." She took a bite of carrot and ignored him.

"Hot and spicy, just the way I like 'em." He laughed at his own joke while she rolled her eyes at him. "It was a joke. What is your problem with me? I'm just trying to be friendly."

"Then don't try. You may have Tamara fooled, but I know who and what you are. If you like this table so much, you can have it. I've lost my appetite."

Alicia got up from the table. She was not spending her lunch hour sitting here playing word games with this jerk. He reached out and caught her arm to stop her.

"I'd like to be your friend." His eyes conveyed exactly what the word friend entailed as he caressed her arm with his other hand.

"I have enough friends, not to mention the fact I find you repulsive. Let go of my arm or you will have a lap full of soup."

Franco came out of nowhere and grabbed Nathan out of his chair. Behind him stood two football jocks with arms folded.

"I don't know what game you think you're playing, but stay away from Alicia. Go find yourself some other unsuspecting victim, like Tamara." Nathan backed down and walked away.

"You can take off the cape today. I don't need you fighting my battles Franco. I can handle Nathan."

"A simple thank you would suffice. Why do I even bother?" Franco turned and stalked out of the cafeteria.

***

She sat on the steps waiting for her father to pick her up from school. He left a message on her cell phone letting her know he was running late.

"Hey," said Franco sitting down beside her. "What are you still doing here?"

"My father is running late. He should be here in about fifteen minutes or so."

"I'll wait with you," he volunteered setting his books down on the step beside him. "I don't like the idea of you being out here alone. You never know when Nathan may pop up."

"About yesterday in the cafeteria," she said softly, "I'm sorry for jumping down your throat. Thanks for rescuing this damsel in distress."

"You're welcome." He smiled. "Now thank me properly."

Alicia was a bit surprised when he leaned over and kissed her lightly on the lips. Her mind was in overdrive. This was her first kiss and she didn't have time to prepare for it.

When she didn't resist, he kissed her again. Shyly, they moved a safe distance away from each other as her father's car pulled up in front of the school.

To say her father was not pleased to see Franco waiting with her was an understatement. Alicia introduced Franco to her father. She explained to him Franco did not want to leave her waiting alone. She told him Franco missed his bus to stay with her.

"Franco hop in," said Miguel Perez kindly. "We'll give you a lift home." Alicia smiled with delight while Franco seemed apprehensive.

"It's no problem sir," said Franco nervously. "I can take the bus home."

"Nonsense. Get in," said her father firmly. He saw the way his daughter was looking at Franco and wanted to find out more about him.

She didn't realize Franco was ashamed of where he lived. She loved her father dearly for easing Franco's mind by telling him about his humble beginnings in Mexico.

Franco's family lived in a two-bedroom apartment in a not so nice neighborhood. The apartment housed five members of the Morales family.

When the car pulled into the parking lot at the apartment complex, Franco got out quickly. He was sweating under Alicia's dad direct stare.

"Thank you Mr. Perez. Alicia, I'll see you at school tomorrow."

"By Franco, " smiled Alicia watching him walk away.

Seeing the smitten look on his daughter's face, Miguel killed the engine and got out of the car. Alicia followed him as he followed Franco.

"Dad where are we going?" she asked running to keep up with him. She followed him to Franco's door. Her mouth fell open when he rang the doorbell. "What are you doing?"

"I'm meeting your boyfriends parent's," said her father watching her face. Her mouth formed an "o".

"But Franco's not my. . ." Her sentence trailed off as Franco opened the door. He stared at her and her father in surprise. "My father wants to meet your parents."

Wordlessly Franco opened the door and stepped back for them to enter the small, but tidy apartment. There was a tense few moments while the parent's were being introduced, but it lasted all of a few seconds.

To the teenager's delight, the father's got along well. Mr. Morales even invited them to stay for dinner. They had to decline because Abuela and Joseph were waiting for them.

During summer break, the families would get together at least once a month so the kids could see each other in a supervised environment. They talked every day on the phone. Miguel Perez even helped Franco's father get on at Sims Electronic.

She didn't see Rainey or Tamara during the summer. Rainey went to Florida to visit her father and Tamara went to New York to spend the summer with her Aunt.

To Alicia's delight, the Morales' bought a home about three blocks over from where she lived. Her Abuela, father, and younger brother all adored Franco.

She looked forward to school starting so she could see Franco everyday. It turned out they had two classes together.

One day after school, they went to the mall and bought matching silver purity rings. They were hearts with a cross inside. In a private ceremony, they slid on each other's rings pledging their hearts to each other. They also pledged to remove the rings together on their wedding night.

She was at her locker, when Nathan leaned against the locker in front of hers. Alicia ignored him. He grabbed her and kissed her.

Alicia pushed him away and slapped him. She had no idea Tamara was standing behind her. She would never forget the look on Tamara's face.

"I always knew you were a creep," seethed Alicia wiping her mouth with the back of her hand. "You are despicable."

"Is that why you keep coming on to me Alicia? Tamara, tell your friend to keep her hands and lips to herself."

You've got to be kidding me. If you dropped dead in front of me, I wouldn't put my mouth on you to recessitate you. I'd save a dog first." She turned to face her silent friend. "Please tell me you are smart enough not to buy into this pack of lies."

"She was all over me, baby," he lied convincingly. "You saw it with your own eyes. You know how competitive she is about everything. You have me and she wants me, but only to win the game."

"You're a lousy actor Nathan. You're wasting your time with those drama classes. Save your breath. Tamara saw what you wanted her to see. She is too good for you. Anyone walking, talking and breathing is too good for you."

"What's going on?" asked Franco looking from Alicia's angry face to Tamara who was on the verge of tears. "What happened?" he repeated.

"This jerk kissed me and now he's trying to get Tamara to believe I kissed him. I wouldn't spit on him if he were on fire."

"You kissed Alicia," Franco hissed grabbing Nathan and slamming him against the locker. Alicia jumped back in surprise at the anger she was witnessing in her boyfriend. She had yet to hear him raise his voice with anyone. "Do you have a death wish today playboy? I warned you once before to stay clear of my girlfriend. Three strikes and you're out."

"Franco let him go," Tamara ordered." Franco shoved Nathan aside and she moving in front of Nathan to shield him with her body. "This is not Nathan's fault. Alicia always has to win at everything. Alicia how could you do this to me? You are supposed to be my friend."

"I am your friend and I am insulted you would believe him," she shot back. "Have I ever lied to you about anything?"

"There's always a first time. You can't stand the fact I'm happy or that Nathan wants me and not you."

"He wants you," she laughed without humor. "Like he's wanted half the Junior

Class. Tamara wake up. He's using you. Once he gets you in the back seat of his convertible, it's bye bye Tamara on the next victim. Are you blind or just stupid?"

Tamara charged and Franco stepped between the two girls. He was not going to let them come to blows over a jerk like Nathan.

"Tamara, use your head and not other parts of your anatomy. There is no way Alicia would kiss Nathan. She despises him. He came onto her a few weeks ago in the cafeteria."

"That's what you keep telling yourself Franco and maybe you'll start to believe it. Maybe she's tired of you professor."

"Even if she were, I doubt she'd come looking for you in Special Ed. Come near Alicia again I will personally rip your head off." He turned his attention back to Tamara. "Who are you going to believe Tamara, this lying creep or your best friend?"

"Come on baby. You don't need them. You have me now. Maybe it's time you made some new friends." He put his arm around her and started to lead her away.

"Don't do it Tamara," warned Alicia. "If you walk away with him, our friendship is over. I mean it." Smugly Nathan led her away. "I can't believe she left with him. She chose that lying cheating manipulating creep over me. She threw our friendship of ten years way just like that," fumed Alicia snapping her fingers. "How could she do it?"

"Love is blind or so they say. Give her some time to come to her senses. You were wrong to give her an ultimatum. Alicia when you back people in a corner, they come out fighting. You were both wrong. Just give it some time. When she finally sees him for who he really is, she's going to need her friends."

"Well she can count me out," said Alicia slamming her locker shut. "Our friendship is over. She made her choice and it wasn't me."

"Why are you so stubborn? Nathan is not worth losing your best friend over."

"Tell that to Tamara," she snapped walking away.

***

She hadn't seen Rainey since she was kicked out of Hockadell. She called her and told her what happened with Tamara. Rainey told her Nathan was a creep and Tamara was blind not to see past a nice pair of biceps.

They hung up agreeing to get together soon. Alicia prayed her friend would wake up and break her ties to Zeke and his group before it was too late.

A week later, Alicia heard Tamara caught Nathan with another girl at the football game. A fight broke out and they were all escorted from the premises.

She also found out from Franco, Nathan broke up their friendship on a bet. He wanted her to talk to Tamara, but she refused. There was no going back.

Two weeks before Alicia's sixteenth birthday, she and Franco decided they couldn't wait. They wanted to make love now. They made plans to meet at Franco's house after school.

Alicia went shopping for the perfect outfit. She wanted Franco to see her not as a girl, but as a woman. The dress bought was totally out of character for her. Franco was in for a surprise.

Abuela would never have let her out of the house wearing the form fitting red knit dress. If her father saw her appearance, he would probably send her off to a convent.

Lucky for her Abuela was out and Joseph was at soccer practice. She stared at her reflection in the mirror hardly recognizing the girl who looked back at her. As an after thought, she applied some make-up. She let down her hair and curled it with the curling iron.

This was only the second time she had ever used the darned thing. Rainey bought it for her last year and showed her how to curl her hair.

Alicia walked the short distance to Franco house and looked down at her watch. She rung the doorbell, but there was no answer. She nervously and impatiently waited for him to answer the door.

She felt a chill go down her spine and froze. Something inside her told her to leave, but she didn't listen.

When the door opened, she frowned when Franco's eighteen-year old brother, Hector opened the door. She'd never felt comfortable around Hector. He didn't do or say anything to make her feel this way, but she felt uneasy with him.

"Come in," he said stepping back for her to enter the house. Folding her hands together nervously, she stepped inside. She looked around for Franco, but he was nowhere in sight. "Franco's not home yet."

Alicia sat on the sofa crossing and uncrossing her legs. She nervously pulled at her short mini dress.

"Did Franco say what time he'd be here?" she asked nervously wetting her dry lips. The way he was looking at her made her uncomfortable.

"No, but as hot as you look, I'm sure he won't be long. You look great."

"Thank you." Alicia got to her feet. "Tell Franco I came by. I can drop back by later."

"Nonsense," smiled Hector. "You stay. I'm going. I'm taking a quick shower and then leaving. I have a date."

Alicia breathed a sigh of relief when he left the room. She got to her feet again. Things were not going according to plan. She looked down at her watch. Franco should have been there by now. Maybe this wasn't meant to be.

I'm sorry Franco, but I'm not ready for this. This is a mistake. I do want to wait until we're married. I want the first time to be special for both of us.

Her mind was made up as she headed for the front door. She opened the door and let out a startled squeal when it was slammed shut.

Her eyes grew round as saucers as they took in the towel clad form of Hector. He leaned in close to her and smelled her hair.

Looking up at him, she tried to put on a brave front. She didn't want him to see how terrified she was.

"I forgot to tell you Franco is in detention until four o'clock."

His hot breath fanned her cheeks and fear raced down her spine at the implication of being very alone with him. She took a step back from him and stared up at him.

"We're all alone little Alicia," he smiled advancing on her. She backed away. "So what do you think we should do to entertain ourselves. If I didn't know any better, I'd say you came here today to lose your virginity." He grabbed her and pulled her flush against him. "And so you shall my beauty."

Before she could react, he grabbed her and pulled her into his arms. Hector kissed her as she struggled in his arms. Freeing her mouth from his, she spit in his face. He released her abruptly and slapped her sending her reeling into the door. She groped for the handle, but he grabbed her before she could open it. She screamed as he caught a handful of her hair and pulled her to him. His hand covered her mouth to drown out her screams and he drug her kicking and clawing to his bedroom.

Fear like nothing she had ever known gripped her as he threw her on the bed. She tried to roll away, but his body stopped her as he fell on top of her.

"Please let me go," she begged fighting him. "Don't do this. Franco will kill you for this. My father will kill you for this."

"I'm not going to tell them. Are you? Who do you think they will believe? You came here for action and that's what you're getting, just not with the brother you were hoping for."

Alicia fought him as he tried to push her dress up. The sounds of muffled screams and tearing clothing filled the air. Her struggles earned her countless bruises all over her body as he tried to make her hold still.

In the end, all her fighting was in vain; brute strength won out and her mind shut down. Her mind tried to block out the ugly truth about what was happening to her. She could hardly breathe as his hand tightened on her throat. She didn't want to breathe. She wanted to die. The pain and the humiliation were more than she could stand. She prayed for death as he used her.

When he was finally finished, he took the purity ring from her finger. She watched in horror as he added to a collection of about five others on a chain around his neck.

"You won't be needing this little gem. Isn't this what you wanted Alicia? You wanted to now what it was like to be a woman. So now, you know. This is your fault. You came looking for sex and that's what you got baby. Was it what you expected?" He grabbed her by the hair and pulled her face close to his. "If you tell anyone I did this to you, I'll kill you." He released her abruptly.

Alicia said nothing as he rolled away from her. Alicia watched him leave the room and she pulled herself into a sitting position. She stumbled as she got to her feet. She kneeled down and picked up her backpack from the floor. She put on a baseball cap to shield her face. Fixing her clothing the best she could, she staggered from the room.

She looked down at her shaking hands. There was blood under her nails to match the scratches on her attackers face and shoulders.

The front door banged against the wall as she ran out. Alicia didn't know or care where she was going. She walked around for what seemed like hours and ignored the ringing cell phone in her purse.

Alicia didn't want to talk to anyone. She knew her Abuela was probably worried about her, but she couldn't go home. She was too ashamed to face her family.

Hector was right. This was her fault. She blamed herself for what happened. She went to Franco's house with the intention of losing her virginity and that's exactly what happened. God was punishing her for planning to do something she knew in her heart was wrong. She put herself in that position. She should have had better judgment and she should have gone home when she had the chance. Now she had to face the consequences of her actions.

Who can I tell? Who will believe me? Was this really my fault? I didn't ask to be raped!

That's not why I went there. Is this my punishment for going there?

She found herself at the tree house staring up. Alicia had no idea why she was here, but something drew her here tonight.

The tree house was her refuge. This is where she came when her mother died. This is where she felt safe.

She climbed the ladder and opened the door. Easing inside the empty tree house, she lay down on the mat covered floor and cried herself to sleep.

Alicia woke with a start when she heard footsteps on the ladder. Hugging herself into a tight ball, she held her breath as she waited. Her entire body was trembling in fear.

When Tamara's head popped in the door, she let out the breath she was holding. Her body relaxed and she closed her eyes in relief. She didn't know whom she was expecting, but it wasn't Tamara.

Tamara looked at her in surprise, but didn't say anything. She moved to a corner of the room and sat down removing her backpack from her shoulder.

They stared at each other, neither willing
to break the silence barrier. The minutes ticked
by until they heard footsteps on the ladder.
Rainey coming inside made the trio complete.

"Don't you see? It's all my fault," Alicia
cried. "I went there to have sex and I did,
although it wasn't with the person I wanted it
to be with. I guess that's my punishment for
thinking about doing it. I went there for sex. I
just got more than I bargained for."

"No, Alicia, this is not your fault," Tamara
denied vehemently. "You are not to blame for
what that pig did to you. You need to go to the
police. You need to press charges against him."

"I can't do that," she cried. "I went there
all dolled up like a happy hooker. This is my
punishment!"

"Alicia, Tamara's right," Rainey said
softly. "This is not your fault. That monster
raped you. You have to tell someone. You
can't let him get away with what he did to
you."

"I don't have a choice. I can't tell my
father or Franco. I don't even know how I can
ever face either one of them again. You didn't
see what I was wearing. I shouldn't have gone

there. My instincts told me to leave and I didn't. I didn't trust my instincts. I put myself in that situation by going there and I only have myself to blame for what happened."

"Did you scream? Did you fight him?" Alicia nodded as tears poured down her face. "Then it's not your fault!" Tamara yelled at her. "You did nothing wrong!"

"I wish I could believe that."

"Believe it," Rainey said squeezing her hand. "You should go to the police. We'll go with you. You have to turn him in. You said he had a collection of rings, which means you were not the first. Who was? Was it one of their sister's friends? My God Maria is only twelve years old. You can't let this go. He has to pay. If you say nothing and do nothing, what's going to stop him from doing this to someone else or from coming after you again?"

"I'll kill myself," Alicia vowed as tears poured down her face. "I would rather die than let him touch me again."

"Then let's go to the police," Tamara said getting to her feet. "You have to stop him. You are the only one who can." Tamara held out her hand to Alicia. Tentatively she caught it and came to her feet. They all embraced each other with tears on their faces. "We are here for you Alicia as long as you need us."

"Let's go," Rainey said moving towards the door. She was moving down the stairs when she swayed. She stopped and gripped the ladder.

Her vision started to fade and she felt herself falling. She thought she heard screams as she landed with a thud on the ground.

Tamara and Alicia screamed when they say Rainey falling. They were still in the tree house and there was nothing they could do to break her fall.

They hurried down the stairs to her side. Dropping down on the ground beside her, they immediately noticed the blood on her pants.

Alicia's pulled her cell phone out of her purse and called 911. Tamara ran to the house to tell her mother and to bring back the paramedics.

"Rainey, can you hear me?" asked a panicked Alicia leaning over her. She checked her pulse and fear set in at how faint it was. "Rainey stay with me. You have to hold on!

You have to fight! The ambulance will be here soon. Please don't leave us."

Chapter 5

Face The Music

Everything after that was a blur as the ambulance arrived and took Rainey. Tamara and Alicia had to confess about Rainey's abortion to the paramedics.

Mrs. Sims drove the girls to the hospital. On the way, she called Rainey's mother to let her know Rainey was being rushed to the hospital.

The next few hours were a nightmare for all of them. The emergency room nurse phoned the police about Rainey's illegal abortion.

The police were there within half an hour. When they walked towards the girls, Alicia froze up.

"I'm officer Jacobs and this is my partner officer Whitmore. We'd like to ask you girls some questions about what happened."

"I'm Janet Sims, " said Janet stepping up and offering her hand. " This is my daughter Tamara and her friend Alicia Perez."

"Mrs. Sims what exactly happened? We were informed Ms. Michael's had an illegal abortion. We need any information you can give us."

"We don't have any details," said Tamara finding her voice. "The only thing we know for sure is Zeke Morgan, Rainey's boyfriend took her somewhere on the south side tonight."

"Do you know where this Morgan boy lives?"

"In Plano, I think. If you run a police check on him, you'll find he has a rap sheet," Tamara threw in.

"Miss you've been awful quiet," said officer Whitmore turning to Alicia. "Do you want to tell us what happened to your face?"

"I fell," Alicia nervously lied taking a step back from the group.

"Can you excuse us for a minute." Tamara caught her arm and pulled her out of earshot. "Don't do this Alicia. Here is your chance to tell them what Hector did to you. You have to tell them the truth. Do it for yourself? Do it for Rainey? We were on our way there when this happened."

"I'm ashamed," Alicia cried hugging her arms to her. "I can't do it. I'm not strong enough."

"Yes you are," said Tamara hugging her. "You are the strongest person I know. You are a fighter. You stand up for yourself and for what you believe in. Don't let him take that way from you. Don't let him win."

Putting on a brave front, Alicia walked over to the policeman. Janet Sims came to stand next to them to find out what was going on.

"I'm ready to make a statement. I was raped today," said the trembling voice. "My rapist name is Hector Morales."

"Oh my God," cried Janet moving to stand next to Alicia. Alicia burst into tears and Janet pulled her into her arms. "Oh sweetie, I'm so sorry."

"I'll be back in a few minutes. Please keep her right here," the police instructed to Janet. She nodded in understanding. He returned minutes later and he was not alone.

"Mrs. Sims, this is Dr. Green. We need to take Miss Perez back for an examination. Can you notify her father, she's here?"

Janet nodded past the lump in her throat as she watched them lead Alicia way. Covering her face with her hands, she took a deep breath to get control of her emotions.

***

Alicia and the policeman followed Dr. Green down the hospital corridor. She found an open room and motioned them inside.

"Normally we do this at other facilities, " said the policeman, "but since you are already here, we've gotten the go ahead to let Dr. Green perform an examination. In a few minutes a female police officer will arrive to take over for me."

Alicia said nothing as she sat on the hospital bed. Her arms protectively hugged her bruised body. The policeman left the room followed by the doctor.

Alone, Alicia stared up at the ceiling. Her hand gripped the gold cross around her throat. She held on to it like it was her lifeline.

God, please give me the strength and courage to get through this. I can't do it alone. I need your love and your strength to see me through. Also, give my family the strength they will need for what is to come. Please bless and protect Rainey. She needs you right now as much as I do.

The door opening interrupted her prayer. Dr. Green and a female policewoman came into the room.

"Alicia I need to explain the procedure to you," said Dr. Green sitting down in the chair beside the bed. "I have to do an internal exam." Alicia cringed at the thought of anyone touching her there again. "I'll be as gentle as I possibly can. I have to ask you some questions first. Were you a virgin?" Alicia nodded not trusting her voice to speak. "I'll do my exam first and then Officer Turner will collect the evidence. She will take pictures of your bruises. When we're finished, you will be allowed to take a shower. You can step behind the screen and change into the hospital gown."

Alicia's hand was shaking as she took the gown. She eased off the bed and moved behind the screen. She took off her clothes and slipped on her gown.

The policewoman had gloves on. She took all her clothes and put them in a plastic bag. Everything she wore was evidence.

Her teeth were rattling and she was shaking as she got up on the bed. Lying back, the doctor asked her to slide all the way down and put her feet in the stirrups. Alicia closed her eyes and pretended she was anywhere but there.

Her humiliation was just beginning as she was poked, prodded, and photographed. They scraped the skin and blood fragments from beneath her fingernails. Everything was bagged as tagged as they went.

How had it all come to this? How could this have happened to me? I'm a good kid. I'm an honor student. I don't lie, cheat, or steal, so why am I being punished. What did I ever do to deserve something like this?

Once the examination was complete, they told her she could take a shower. Because Hector used a condom, no semen was present.

Alicia moved slowly as she got off the bed. The doctor's wanted to keep her a couple of hours just for observation. She sat on the floor is the shower hugging her arms to her body.

When she came back into the room, the doctor was back. She pulled back the covers for Alicia to ease back into bed.

"Your father has been contacted. He should be here shortly. Is there anything I can get for you? Do you need something to eat or drink?"

Alicia shook her head in refusal. Her father was on his way to the hospital. This made the floodgate of tears start again. She was not ready to face her father.

Dr. Green held a syringe in her hand. She told Alicia she was going to give her something to relax her and help her rest.

***

Janet Sims called Alicia's father and told him to come to the hospital. She couldn't bring herself to tell him what had happened to his daughter either. She could hardly believe it herself.

Tamara and her mother sat in the waiting room praying for both girls. Because they were not family, the nurse couldn't tell them anything.

Rainey's mom was the first one to arrive. She was a nervous wreck when she got there. She ran over to Janet and Tamara.

"What happened to Rainey?" she asked terrified. "Where is she? Please tell me she's not. ." She couldn't bring herself to say the word.

Janet put her arm around Shannon and led her to the back of the room and away from prying eyes and ears.

"Rainey had an abortion tonight." Shannon staggered and Janet caught her. "She went to some clinic in Oak Cliff. She was at the tree house with Alicia and Tamara and started hemorrhaging. The girls called 911 and the ambulance brought her here."

"Rainey had an abortion. No," said Shannon shaking her head. "That's not possible. I would know if my daughter was pregnant. I should know. There's been a mistake."

Shannon broke down in Janet's arms. She blamed herself for not being there to take care of her daughter. When she gathered herself together, she went to the nurse and asked if there was any word on Rainey's condition. The nurse told her no and gave her the necessary paperwork to fill out.

She called Rainey's dad and told him what was going on. He said he'd be on the next plane to Dallas.

They were all on pins and needles when a doctor walked over to them. He sat down across from Shannon.

"Mrs. Michael's, I'm Dr. Patterson. My colleague Dr. Hunter is prepping Rainey for surgery." Shannon gripped Janet's hand. "Rainey's has a perforated uterus as a result of the abortion. We have to perform an emergency hysterectomy to save her life."

"Oh God!" cried Shannon in pain. "Is there any other way? Would another procedure work? Anything, but this."

"I'm afraid not. We have tried everything we know. This is the last result. I'll come out and let you know when the operation is over."

Shannon was beside herself with pain, fear, and anger. She wanted answers. She wanted to know how this happened and who butchered her daughter.

"What do you know about this Tamara?" she asked turning to face Tamara. "Did you know Rainey was pregnant?"

"No. Rainey and I aren't exactly friends anymore. We haven't spoken in months. She came to the tree house tonight after the abortion."

"Shannon, Tamara and Alicia gave the police their statement. They went to pick up Zeke Morgan to find out where he took Rainey."

"I told her he was trouble. I warned her to stay away from him. How could she do something like? How do I tell my daughter if she makes it through the surgery, she will never have kids?"

Tamara was crying too. She couldn't believe any of this was happening. Rainey was in their fighting for her life because she made the wrong decision. Poor Rainey this news was going to be devastating for her.

Tamara prayed for both her friends while her mother filled in Shannon about Alicia. Shannon was mortified.

She sat there not saying as word as her mother filled her in on what happened to Alicia.

Miguel Perez came through the emergency room doors and stopped when he saw them. He looked at their faces in fear.

"Where's Alicia?" he asked with dread. "Shannon what happened to my daughter?"

"Miguel," said Shannon past the lump in
her throat. She got to her feet and walked
towards him, "Alicia was raped."

They all watched the color leave his face
and he stumbled. Shannon caught him before
he fell. His face was etched with pain and
disbelief.

"Mr. Perez we need to speak with you,"
said the policeman leading a broken Miguel
away from the women.

They watched as the policeman talked to
him. When he hit the wall with his fist, they all
jumped.

Miguel came charging towards the door
with murder in his eyes. Janet and Shannon
flanked him. Shannon stepped in front of him
placing her hands on his chest.

"Move out of the way Shannon. This does
not concern you. That animal hurt my baby. He
will pay for it."

"You are not going anywhere. Alicia needs
you. If you go after the man who did this,
where does that leave your daughter? Let the
police handle it." Some of the fight went out of
him. "Our children need us right now. We have
to be here for them. If you go to jail what

happens to Alicia and Joseph. What happens to us?" she asked softly. "I love you. I will not lose you this way."

He closed his eyes pulling her into his arms. He held her and they both cried. Sitting down, Shannon told him about Rainey. They had no idea how they were going to get through the next 48 hours with their daughters or without each other.

Tamara and her mother did a double take. They had no idea Alicia and Rainey's parents were involved and neither did the girls.

Once Miguel was calm, the police officer came and got him. He led him through the double doors to see Alicia.

Shannon asked Janet and Tamara not to mention their relationship until they have a chance to tell Rainey and Alicia. She promised they would tell them eventually, but now was not the right time.

***

Alicia was nervously fingering the covers when the door opened and her father stepped inside the room. He rushed to the bed and took his battered and bruised only daughter in his arms. He held her tightly as they both cried.

"Oh mija, I'm so sorry," he said hugging her close. "I should have been there to protect you. I let you down."

"Poppy, I'm the one who's sorry," she cried returning his hug. "This is not your fault. It's mine. I let this happen to me. I should have fought harder. I shouldn't have been there in the first place. I brought this on myself." He framed her bruised face gently in his hands.

"No sweetheart," he said shaking his head. "Don't ever think that. This is not your fault. The fault lies with the animal that did this to you. He will pay with his life. Tell me who did this?"

"No Poppy," she said adamantly shaking her head. "Let the police handle it. I can't lose you. I need you. Joseph needs you."

"Ssh calm yourself. The doctor said I could take you home in a few hours. You need to lay back and rest. Your body needs time to heal." He kissed her forehead. She gripped him hand. "I promise I will be here when you wake up. I'm not going any where."

"I love you daddy," her eyes fluttered shut as the shot took effect. Alicia settled back against the pillows and drifted off the sleep. In her dreams, it was happening all over again. Hector was there leering down at her. He was tearing at her clothes and laughing at her. Alicia woke up screaming.

Her father was there to soothe her and get her back to sleep. He climbed onto the bed and held her in the protective cocoon of his arms. His tears wet her hair as he cried silent tears.

***

Shannon and the others waited anxiously for Rainey's surgery to be over. When the doctor came out, she rushed to him.

"How's my daughter? Please tell me she made it through the surgery?"

"She made it. She's stable right now. We'll be moving her to recovery. After we get her settled, you can see her."

"Thank God." She sagged against Janet in relief.

"We stopped the bleeding, but she's in bad shape. We almost lost her on the table. It's going to take a while for her to recover. When she comes too, the police are going to want to talk to her about where she had the abortion. She's a very lucky young woman. A few minutes more and she would have bled to death."

Tamara was numb as she listened to the doctor. Rainey almost died. Alicia's quick thinking saved her life. She turned towards the door and wondered what was happening with Alicia. Alicia was brutally raped by her boyfriend's brother. Would she ever be able to get past it?

Her own immortality was staring her in the face. If Cindy could be believed, there was a chance she could have AIDS.

She didn't blame it on the ripped condom anymore. She blamed herself and her lack of judgment.

Tamara knew she wasn't ready to take that step and she did it to save her relationship with Rodney. She now realized they didn't have a relationship. He had used her the same way he had used countless other girls.

She hugged her arms to her body protectively as she watched her mother try and comfort Rainey's mother.

Who would comfort her parent's if she died? Would her little brother even remember her ten years from now? What had she really accomplished in her short lifetime? How could she have been so stupid?

When her father walked through the emergency door, Tamara ran to him. He held her in his arms as she cried.

She didn't realize how lucky she was to have a mother and father who were still together until now. She knew her parents loved her unconditionally and would protect her with their last breath.

Up to this point, she took her life for granted. Now that life could be slipping away from her and her father's money couldn't save her.

"Sweetheart it's going to be okay," reassured her father hugging her. "You'll see. It will all work itself out. Alicia and Rainey will get through this."

"It will never be okay," Tamara cried shaking her head. "Nothing will ever be right again. This is not fair. Why are we all being punished?"

Her mother walked over and put her arms around both of them. She didn't say anything. She just held them.

They sat in the waiting room while
Rainey's mom was led back to recovery.
Watching Mrs. Michaels, Tamara made the
decision to tell her parents the truth.

***

Rainey was drowsy and barely conscious
when her mother came into the recovery room.
She tried to speak, but no words came. Her
throat was too dry to talk and she could barely
keep her eyes open.

"Ssh, don't say anything," her mother said
taking her hand. She sat down in the chair
beside the bed. "Let me talk, sweetie. I'm so
sorry I wasn't there for you. I was so caught up
in my job I neglected you. I should have been
there for you. Honey you should have been
able to tell me anything. I'm sorry you didn't
feel you could tell me you were pregnant."

Tears poured down Rainey's face as she
stared at her mom's tortured face. She wanted
to tell her mother it wasn't her fault, but she
couldn't. Part of her did resent all the time her
mother spent at work and how little time she
spent with her. Her mother gave her too much
freedom. She knew it wasn't her mother's fault
she got pregnant. No one told her to sleep with

Zeke and no one made her have an abortion.
The choice was hers.

As her eyes fluttered closed, she had no
idea what happened to her. The last thing she
remembered was climbing down the ladder at
the tree house.

"Rest baby. I'll be right here when you
wake up. Mommy's not going anywhere. I love
you sweetheart."

I love you too mom.

***

Tamara and her parent's were still waiting
in the lobby, when Rainey's dad got there.
They took him aside and Janet told him what
happened.

Tamara would never forget the look on his
face; the pain and the disappointment were
there in his blue eyes.

He went to the front desk and they buzzed
the nurse. Mr. Michael's was led back to
Rainey's room.

"Let's go home," said Janet Sims coming
to her feet. "I think Shannon and Ken need
some time alone with Rainey. Shannon will
call if she needs anything."

"Mom, I'd like to find out about Alicia before we leave," said Tamara twisting her hands. "Please." Her mother led her over to the nurse's station. "Is there any information on Alicia Perez? Is she being released tonight?"

"I'm sorry I can't give out that information," the nurse said apologetically.

"Her father is with her. Can you ask him to come out and see Tamara Sims?"

"Sure. I'll buzz the back and have someone get him."

Tamara and her parents waited for Miguel Perez. Minutes later when he came out the door, he looked at least ten years older than when he went inside.

"How's Alicia?" Tamara asked wringing her hands.

"As well as could be expected," he said running his hands through his hair. "The doctor gave her a sedative to help her rest."

"Miguel take all the time you need," said Thomas Sims. "If there's anything we can do, please call us."

"Thanks. I'd better get back to Alicia. I'll tell her you asked about her, Tamara." They sadly watched him go through the double doors.

"Come on, let's get you home," said Thomas Sims putting his arm around his daughter. He ushered her out the emergency room doors.

When they arrived home, her mother ran her a nice relaxing bath. Tamara reflected on everything that happened today. Her day had gone from bad to worse, first Rodney, then Rainey and now Alicia. All the lies and secrets brought them to where they were today. Rainey should have confided her pregnancy to her mother. Alicia should never have gone to Franco's house. She wasn't ready for sex. None of us were ready and look where it's landed us. We all should have waited.

Tamara knew she had to tell her parents the truth. She knew they would be hurt and disappointed, but she owed it to them to tell them the truth.

She knocked hesitantly on their bedroom door. Her father bid her enter. She took a deep calming breath before walking in. She stood at the foot of the bed clasping her hands together in front of her.

"Mom, dad, there's something I have to tell you," she said nervously. Her parents waited expectantly for her to go on. "I had a boyfriend named Rodney. A couple of times a week, I would skip drill team practice and go to his parent's house with him." She heard her mother's sharp intake of breath, but she couldn't look up at her. Instead, she looked down at her hands. "This went on for a couple of weeks. We didn't do anything other than fool around at first. He started pressuring me to have sex. I told him no and stopped seeing him." She stopped and took a deep breath. "Then one day I saw him in the hallway flirting with another girl. I became jealous and lost my head." Her eyes met her parents. "I slept with him to keep him. I know it was a stupid thing to do. I know what you're going to say and I'll save you the trouble. I made a mistake. I should have waited. I shouldn't have fallen for his lies, but I did."

"Please tell us you're not pregnant," whispered her mother wiping her tears. "You're only fifteen years old. At your age, sex was the last thing on my mind."

"No mom. I'm not pregnant. There are worse things," she said softly. She wet her dry lips. "Rodney used a condom, but it tore. I've had my cycle so I know I'm not pregnant."

"Thank God," added her father. "Why are you telling us this now? There's more isn't there?"

"As I stated before, there are worse things than being pregnant. A girl he slept with before me has a sexual partner who is HIV positive." She stopped at her mother's loud gasp. "Mom I fainted because I overheard her tell him he needed to be tested along with anyone else he slept with. The doctor's office ran an HIV test on me. I'm waiting for the results."

Her parents sat staring at her speechless. Tamara was unnerved by their silence. This is not the reaction she expected. She expected crying on her mother's part and yelling from her father.

The tears started to fall again, when her mother held out her arms to her. Crying she ran to her mother's waiting arms. Her father hugged both of them and they all cried together.

Like she did when she was a frightened child, she got in bed between her parents. They talked for hours about her situation. Her father also gave her a stern lecture about not only safe sex, but about abstinence.

Her father decided to take some time off from work so the family could spend some quality time together. He made the remark about it always being a tragedy before people realize how important their families are. He promised to do better with both his children.

Her mother also agreed to cut back on her hours at the Teen shelter and spend more time with her. Janet Sims spent countless hours helping other teens with their problems, when her own daughter didn't feel she could confide in her. This gave her a moment of pause. It made her question how effective she really was at the shelter.

Lying in bed, her father switched over to the news station. They were all speechless by the news report. Her father turned to his daughter. Tamara was pale and shaking. The nightmare wasn't over yet. There was more to come.

The news report stated there was a shooting on the 4000 Block of Audelia. The police were there to make an arrest and things turned ugly. The report stated a young Hispanic male stabbed his older brother. The younger brother was shot and both brothers were being transported to the hospital.

"Oh God will this nightmare never end," Tamara whispered. "Franco was shot for going after Hector for raping Alicia. Poor Alicia. Will she ever be able to live any of this down? I wonder if she knows about this. Maybe I should call her."

"No," said her father sternly. He picked up the phone and dialed. "Miguel its Thomas Sims. Call me when you get this message."

***

Alicia was slowly coming out of her drug-induced sleep. She looked over to see her father sitting in the chair next to her bed. He was watching the news. She didn't say anything as she watched him. She loved her father so much. She knew this was killing him.

"Late breaking news, I'm Joanna Fairday. The police went to make an arrest in the 4000 block of Audelia and things turned ugly. His younger brother stabbed the man being arrested for sexual assault. The police shot the younger brother and both brothers were being rushed to Medical Center for treatment. The police stated both young men are in good condition."

"Oh God! Franco's been shot!" cried Alicia getting out of bed. She staggered slightly and her father caught her. "I have to see Franco. He needs me."

"No, sweetheart. You need to rest. The report said Franco was fine." He helped her back to the bed.

"No. I want to get dressed and see him. I have to know he's all right. This happened because of me. If I hadn't gone there none of this would have happened."

Miguel knew there was no reasoning with Alicia right now. She was too distraught over everything that happened today. If seeing Franco would help ease her pain, he would take her to see him.

"There's a change of clothes for you in the bathroom. I'll call the front desk and find out if he's been admitted."

"Thanks daddy," she smiled through her tears hugging him. "I love you." Alicia dressed as quickly as she could. When she came back into the room a police officer was with her father.

"Alicia have a seat," said her father. Her heart was in her chest as she walked over to the bed and sat down. She prayed nothing bad had happened to Franco.

"Is it Franco?" She asked past the lump in her throat. "Is he okay? Please don't sit there staring at me. Don't keep me in suspense. What's wrong?"

"Franco is fine," said the policeman, "but you can't see him. He's under arrest. Ms. Perez, he tried to murder his brother."

"His brother raped me! He deserves to die! I hope he dies for what he did to me! That would be justice!"

"Honey calm down. I will help pay for the best defense for Franco." He turned to face the officer. "If I were you, I'd post a guard outside Hectors door or you might find your prisoner dead. It's not a threat. It's a promise. I'll finish what Franco started."

"Both men are under guard. The officer did not shoot to kill. Franco has only a flesh wound. He'll be released in about an hour.

He'll be taken to juvenile detention. Hectors wound is more serious. He'll be released in a couple of days into our custody. A word of warning Mr. Perez, don't take the law into your own hands. He is in police custody now. Let us handle this."

"It's just as well," said Alicia walking over to the window and staring out. "I don't know if I can ever face Franco again. I ruined his life.

***

Rainey came slowly out of her medicated fog. She looked to her right and her mother was sleeping on the couch with a blanket over her. Looking to her left, she saw her father. He was also asleep in a chair by the bed.

She was numb from the waist down. Rainey closed her eyes and tried to remember what happened to her. Painful memories of the abortion hit her like a ton of bricks. She winced in remembrance and her father came awake immediately.

"Hey princess," said her father getting to his feet. He dropped a light kiss on her forehead. "How are you feeling?"

"Drowsy and drugged." She tried to smile. "Do I look as bad as I feel?"

"You look beautiful to me. Do you want me to wake your mom?"

"No," she said softly shaking her head. "She probably needs the rest. She's been putting in a lot of hours at Sims Electronic." She ran her fingers through her long blonde hair. "So what's the prognosis? What happened to me?"

"How much do you remember?" he asked tentatively picking up her limp hand.

"I was in the tree house with Alicia and Tamara. We were talking about things. We were coming down the ladder to go to the police station. Where's Alicia? Is she all right?"

"Alicia's a fighter. I'm sure she'll be fine in time. What about you Rainey? Do you remember what happened to you?"

Rainey nodded past the lump in her throat. She had something right now she didn't have for the past 15 years. She had her father's undivided attention.

"I went to a clinic," said the strained voice. "I had an abortion. I shouldn't have done it. I shouldn't have killed my baby. There were other options. I should have told mom. We could have dealt with this together. I was afraid to tell her because I knew she would be disappointed in me. I made a mess out of everything."

"Rainey, sweetheart," said her mother coming to the side of the bed. She caught her daughter's hand. "What else do you remember?"

"Not much. Before I passed out, there was blood, a lot of blood. I thought I was dying. Was it from the abortion." Her mother nodded and tried to fight back her tears. She looked up at her parents. They were both crying. Dread filled her and she forced the words from her throat. "What happened to me? Why are you two crying?"

"Honey, we're just crying because you're going to be okay," said her mother quickly. "You gave us a scare. You almost died." Her mother looked at her father and he nodded in agreement. "We're just glad you made it through the surgery.

"Why are you two nodding and talking in code? I'm not a child anymore. What surgery?"

she frowned. Again, silence filled the room. "What kind of surgery did I have mom?" She looked curiously from he mother to her father. "What is it you're not telling me? What did they do to me?"

She watched her mother clasp and unclasp her hands. She paced the room wrestling with the decision of whether or not to tell her daughter the truth at this particular time. Shannon didn't want anything to hinder Rainey's recovery.

"Shannon, we owe her the truth. Telling her later as opposed to now is not going to make the telling any easier."

Rainey's hand was cold as ice as her mother caught it and held it between hers. Shannon sat down in the chair by the bed and took a deep breath.

"The nurse who performed the procedure is in police custody. She could have killed you Rainey. You took a dangerous risk and it almost cost you your life. Honey, there shouldn't be anything you can't tell me and talk to me about. I was young once. I remember how it was."

"Mom, you're scaring me. What did they do to me?" she repeated softly. "Tell me."

"During the abortion, the nurse perforated your uterus. The doctor's had to stop the bleeding to save your life. There was only one way to stop it. They had to perform an emergency hysterectomy to save your life."

The rest of Rainey's world fell away and her whole body became numb at her mother's words. Hysterectomy! That meant she could never have kids. The baby she killed would be the only child she would ever have. This was her punishment for taking a life. She would never have the family she one day wanted. She would never be called 'mommy'. She wouldn't be receiving any Mother's Day cards. Her mother and father's arms would never hold a grandchild because of her foolish actions.

Her hand covered her stomach and she began to cry gut-wrenching sobs. She became hysterical and started screaming and pulling at the I.V. in her hand.

While her father held her to keep her from hurting herself. Her mother pushed the button for a nurse. Her parents tearfully watched as the nurse came in and gave her a shot to sedate her.

The nurse phoned the doctor and for the time being, he ordered her to be restrained for her own safety. The nurse strapped her arms and legs to the bed.

Rainey came awake slowly. She tried to raise her arm and couldn't. She frowned and looked over at her hands. They were both in restraints and so were her legs.

She closed her eyes as the previous night came back to haunt her. Rainey remembered everything vividly, the abortion and the news of her hysterectomy. She became hysterical and had to be sedated.

Her parents were back asleep in their perspective beds of choice. Mom was on the couch and dad in the chair.

I'm fifteen years old and I've ruined my life. I feel empty inside. I've done some stupid things in my life, but this one takes the cake. There is no rebounding from this one. There is nothing I can do to change what happened. I can't hit stop and rewind on my life. I'll probably never marry. What man will want a wife who can't bear his children?

The next couple of days, things went down hill. Rainey refused to eat, drink, or speak. Her parents pleaded with her to talk to them, but she slipped further and further into a state of depression.

Her father had to drag her mother from her room to get her to leave Rainey's side. They went to the cafeteria to get a bite to eat.

Rainey willed herself to slip away from reality. She couldn't deal with everything that happened to her. She didn't want to talk or think about it. She felt herself slipping away.

When the door opened, she didn't even bat an eye. She was used to people coming and going. She didn't care anymore. She didn't care about anything.

"Rainey," said Zeke coming further into the room. "What's wrong with you? Why are you strapped to the bed?"

She was groggy from the drugs and thought she imagined him. She blinked several times trying to focus on him.

"I need your help Zeke," said Rainey softly. "I need you to take these bonds off and get me out of here."

He eyed her warily as he approached the bed. He fingered the IV and the straps and shook his head.

"You didn't answer my question. Why are you strapped down? They only do this to crazy people. I can't help you. Hey, I just got out of juvenile detention. I don't need any more trouble because of you."

Her body froze. If she were not strapped down, she would have struck him. How dare he say he didn't need any more trouble because of her? This was all his idea. This was his fault as much as hers. Listening to him and sleeping with him brought her to this low point in her life.

"Get out of my room," she hissed between gritted teeth. "Don't ever come near me again. I listened to you and almost died. Because I was stupid and listened to you, I will never be able to have children. I let you do this to me. I will pay for my stupidity for the rest of my life while you walk away without a scratch."

"No one forced you Rainey. You could have said no. You had a choice."

"You're right. I had a choice and I made the worst possible decision I could have made.

My mother was right about you. Everyone I
know was right about you and I didn't listen.
The blinders are off Zeke. I see you for who
you are and who you've always been. Get out. I
don't ever want to see you again!"

"I know you're upset. When you calm
down, give me a call and we'll get together.
This will all be a bad memory." He touched the
restraint at her wrist and she shrank away from
him.

"Don't touch me! A bad memory for you
maybe, but we are talking about my life. I
would rather lie here strapped down to this bed
than have you ever touch me again. For your
own safety, I would suggest you leave me
strapped in and go. You really don't want my
father to find you here. On second thought,
why don't you stay? I'm sure Dad's looking
forward to meeting you. He could probably
arrange for you to have a room right down the
hall."

***

During the next few weeks, things got back
to normal or as normal as they could get under
the current circumstances. Alicia was back at
school and attending rape counseling sessions

on a regular basis. Her strength and determination to gain back her independence was remarkable. She was slowly coming to grips with what happened and determined not to let it ruin her life. She had a long way to go, but in time, she would get there. Alicia was a fighter.

Franco was released on bail, but lost his scholarship to Hockadell. A silent benefactor paid for his continuing education at another school.

The charges against him were still pending, but Miguel hired him one of the best attorney's money could buy. He was sure under the circumstances Franco would get off with only doing community service.

Hector was in jail without bail. After his arrest, four other girls came forward and admitted he raped them as well. The District Attorney's office assured them with the purity rings as part of the evidence he would not be getting out anytime soon.

Alicia was helping her grandmother with dinner when the doorbell rang. She left the kitchen to answer the door. She opened the door thinking it was Mrs. Taylor dropping off Joseph from soccer practice.

She came up short and froze when she saw Franco standing there. The air left her lungs as she stared at him.

They both shared a lot of guilt about the afternoon she was raped. Alicia blamed herself for going to the house and Franco blamed himself for not being there.

"Hi," said Franco meeting her frantic gaze. "I just came by to see how you were doing. Can I come in for a minute?"

Alicia was trembling as she stepped back for him to enter. Closing the door behind him, she kept a safe distance from him. She unconsciously hugged her arms to her.

This was the first time they were face to face since the rape. She couldn't meet his eyes and him being there made her uncomfortable.

"What are you doing here?' she asked quietly.

"Well since you didn't return any of my calls, I thought I'd drop by." He followed her into the living room. "I'm so sorry for what Hector did to you."

"It's not your fault. You are not your brother's keeper. You are not responsible for what he did."

"Then why do I feel so guilty?" asked the emotional voice. "Why can't you face me? You can't even look at me."

Alicia closed her eyes at the pain in his voice. She didn't want to hurt him, but they couldn't go back. She knew that and she felt in her heart he knew it as well.

He touched her arm and she flinched away from him. Alicia was shaking as she turned around to face him. Tears streamed down her cheeks.

"Why didn't you show up that day? We planned to meet at 3:30 at your parent's house. What kept you?" her voice cracked and she couldn't go on.

"God, Alicia don't you think I haven't been over this is my head a million times. If I could turn back the hands of time, I would." He stopped talking and started pacing. "Rodney and I had an altercation in gym. He said something about you and I slugged him. We were both held in detention until 4:00 P.M. I called your cell phone, but it was off. I called

home and told Hector you were on your way
over. I told him to tell you what happened and
tell you I would call you. I had no idea he was
a rapist. I never would have put you in his path
if I had known."

"I know that," she sniffed. "I know you
would never hurt me. I also know we can't go
back and we can't move forward. I love you
and I know you love me, but I don't know if
we can ever get past this."

"I know. All we can do is take one day at a
time." He turned to walk away. "Take care of
yourself. If you ever need anything, you know
where to find me."

Sadly, she watched him leave. Alicia
dropped down to the sofa numb. As much as
she wanted to reach out to Franco, she
couldn't. She couldn't reach out to anyone.

She was still sitting on the couch when her
father came home from work. He was puzzled
when he saw her staring into space.

"Hey what's wrong?" he asked coming into
the house setting his briefcase by the coffee
table. "You look like you've seen a ghost."

"Franco came by," she softly said not
meeting his eyes. Her father stiffened beside

her, but remained silent. "It wasn't as bad as I expected. I still love him, but I don't think either one of us can get past what happened. He blames himself and I guess a part of me blames him as well. I know it wasn't his fault, but it doesn't change the way I feel."

"I know sweetie," said her father taking her in his arms. "Franco is a good boy and I like him. He's not to blame. There is nothing he could have done to prevent what happened if his brother had already targeted you for his next victim. It could have happened at any time. The fact that you went there does not make you guilty. Honey, don't ever feel guilty or ashamed for what that monster did to you." He raised her face to his. "Being raped does not change what you are in here," he said touching his heart. "I am so proud of you. You have an inner strength that is amazing for one so young. After what you went through some girls, no let me correct myself, some women, would have given up hope. They would have hid inside their homes and let there fear and distrust for people rein, but not my little brave Alicia. You didn't lock yourself away from the world. You faced it head on. When I wanted to send you to another school, you turned me down flat. I was trying to protect you. Your first day back at school, you became my hero. I wanted to walk you inside, but you said no. You said you had to do it alone."

"Not quite alone," she sniffed. "Tamara was waiting for me. She's been a good friend and so has Rainey."

"Changing the subject before we both turn on the water works again," smiled her father wiping his wet cheeks, "do you remember when you told me I need to get a girlfriend." Alicia eyed him warily. "I took your advice."

"You did. That has to be a first," she teased. "So who is she and when do I get to inspect, I mean meet her."

"How about at dinner tonight? She and her daughter are coming for dinner. Why do you think Abuela was preparing so much food? Go get ready."

Alicia was in her room when the doorbell rang. She was smiling as she left the room. She was excited for her father. It was good to see him smile again.

She stood back and watched him primp in the hall mirror. She wondered if he was in love with this woman.

***

Rainey was home alone with her mom. Her father left for Florida a few days ago. Before he left, she got to tell him how she really felt.

She stressed to her father the only time she talked to him on a regular basis was when she was in trouble. She also told him she was not coming back to Florida in the summer unless he took some time off to spend with her.

"Rainey, can we talk?" asked her mother coming into the room. She sat up in bed and turned off the television when her mother sat down on the bed beside her. "You brought up something I think we need to discuss. I'm sorry you had to find out what happened with your father and I threw an overheard argument."

"Did you really get pregnant to trap him into marrying you?"

"Yes I did," she said honestly. "I was young stupid and in love. Ken and I were seniors in high school we were dating exclusively or so I thought. I found out there was another girl. We were both supposed to go away to college, but I messed it all up. I knew if we went to separate colleges, I would lose him, so I did the unthinkable. I stopped taking my birth control pills. I never stopped to consider the long-term consequences of my actions. When I found out I was pregnant, I was so excited, but terrified to tell my parents. I told Ken I was pregnant and he was livid. He accused me of getting pregnant on purpose. Of course, I denied it. He gave me money and told me to go have an abortion. I kept the money and told him I had. I waited until it was too late to have one and then told my parents. They were furious. I was to be the first one in the family to go to college. They went to see Ken's parents and they both decided we had to get married. I was on top of the world. Ken was furious at me. We were married a few weeks later. When you were born, it was the happiest day of my life. I loved you. I cherished you and so did your father. I remember the first time he held you. Years later, I admitted to him what I did. He walked out. He came back eventually, but things had changed. I don't have to tell you we didn't have the fairy tale life or marriage I envisioned. Ken worked nights and went to school during the day to get his degree. After he got his, I went back to school for mine. It wasn't easy, but we both managed to graduate. Your father and I were not happy and when he left, it was like a weight being lifted from both our shoulders. We may not love each other, but we do love you. Don't ever doubt that."

"Thank you for telling me the truth. I know it wasn't easy for you. I love you mom, but you need to spend more time with me. You work all the time and leave me here alone. You tried to give me everything, but what you gave me was too much freedom and not enough parental guidance. I need you mom, now more than ever."

"I know you do and I intend to be here. I'll even go with you to counseling if you need me to. Honey, I'm willing to do whatever I can to help you get through this."

"I feel so empty," said Rainey putting her hand on her stomach. "I'll never get the chance to be a mother. I ruined everything mom."

"No you didn't," said her mother taking her in her arms. "Sweetheart there is more to being a mother than giving birth. Having a child does not make you a mother. Some day you will meet some lucky man and make him a wonderful wife and mother. Don't ever sell yourself short. You have a lot to offer someone. A child does not define who you are. That's something you have to do Rainey. You have got to clean up your act and get on the right track. It's not to late for you."

A few days later, Rainey asked her mother to make an appointment with a psychologist. Shannon was overjoyed her daughter was taking a step in the right direction.

"Rainey, there's something I have to tell you," said Shannon sitting down next to her on the sofa. "I'm seeing someone."

"Mom, that's great. You deserve some happiness. I can tell from that smile on your face this man makes you very happy."

"Yes, he does. You get to meet him tonight. We're having dinner with him and his kids tonight."

"He has kids, great," she said with less enthusiasm. "Just tell me that are not in diapers and I don't have to baby sit."

"No," laughed Shannon. "You won't have to baby sit, much. He has a daughter your age.

I think the two of you will get along famously."

"Famous last words. What time is dinner? I don't have a thing to wear."

"Maybe I can do something about that. Stay right here." Puzzled she watched her mother leave the room. She returned a few minutes later with a garbage bag. "There may be something in there you can wear."

"My things!" She excitedly looked through the bag. "Thank you mom." She laughed hugging her mother. "I promise you won't regret this."

They were in the car when her mother turned on Alicia's street. She frowned and looked at her mother.

"This is Alicia's street." They pulled into the drive at Alicia's house. "Why are we here?"

"I need to drop something off to Miguel before dinner," she said opening the car door. "Come inside and see Alicia."

"Okay," said Rainey getting out of the car and following her mother to the front door. Shannon rang the doorbell.

"Hi, come on in, "said Miguel smiling as he opened the door. He stepped back for them to enter.

"Hi, Mr. P.," said Rainey walking past him to greet Alicia. "Hi squirt." She playfully ruffled Joseph's dark hair. The two girls embraced warmly and started for Alicia's room.

"Wait a minute," said Shannon stopping their hasty exit. She waved both girls over. "Have a seat."

"There something we want to tell you," he paused and caught Shannon's hand, "Shannon and I are in love and we're getting married."

Both girls had a look of total shock on their faces. They stared at their parents and then at either. Their surprised faces moved back to their parents.

The room was so silent you would have heard the proverbial pen drop at their announcement. Silence reigned supreme in the room.

"What does that mean?" asked Joseph breaking the deadly silence. "Are we all gonna live together?"

"Mom! Dad!" the girls chorused finding their voices at last.

"I think they're warming up to the idea, don't you?" asked Shannon kissing Miguel in front of the children.

After the girls got over the initial shock, they were thrilled. They really would be sisters. The Michaels family and the Perez family would become one family.

Miguel and Tamara went out to the backyard to talk, while Shannon spoke with Alicia and Joseph. Joseph was thrilled by the idea of getting a mother. He was only a baby when their mother died.

To everyone's delight, they were planning a May wedding. The wedding preparations took everyone's mind temporarily off their own problems.

Abuela was going to live in New Mexico with Miguel's brother and his wife. He and Shannon talked it over and she was quitting work to stay home and be a full time mother. She was thrilled by the idea.

***

The crisis they all face brought the trio of terror back together. The girls were closer now than they ever had been. They talked every day, sometimes twice a day.

For Tamara, the waiting was the hardest part. She was a nervous wreck as she waited for the results of her HIV test.

Everyone time the phone rang, she jumped a mile and then rushed to answer it. Everyone in the Sims house was on edge.

Her mother and father became her lifeline. They were very supportive and the lines of communication were always open. Tamara spent more time with her brother. They went to the park and for walks. She even took him up in the tree house.

She surprised her mother one day by offering to go with her to the teen shelter. Tamara had been there a few times over the years, but it didn't make an impact on her. Now it did, everything did. She saw first hand the importance of what her mother did for the young girls.

Tamara saw Rodney at school and he tried to talk to her. She blew him off. She had learned a painful lesson with him, one she was not about to repeat.

She grew up a lot in the past few weeks. Gone was the starry eyed innocent little girl who still believed in fairy tales and happily ever after. She was now faced with the hard cruel reality of life. Tamara tried to grow up to fast. She made bad choices and now she had to face the consequences of those choices. Because of her rash actions, her whole life now hung in the balance of one phone call.

Tamara was sitting watching television when the doorbell rang. She got to her feet and went to answer it.

Opening the door, she was surprised to see Rodney. Unlocking the screen, she stood back to allow him to enter the house.

"What are you doing here?" she asked without preamble.

"I came by to talk. I hope I'm not interrupting anything," he said looking around nervously. "If you're busy I can come back."

She eyed him warily. Something was definitely wrong or he wouldn't be here. Rodney was way too uneasy.

"Rodney why don't you have a seat and tell me the reason you're here. You've never been to my home before. As I recall, you avoided it

like the plague. You said you weren't into
parent thing." She waved for him to have a seat
and sat down as well.

"This is not easy for me to say, but I feel I
owe you the truth." He took a deep breath and
met her questioning eyes. "When I gave you
that promise ring, it was from the heart. I love
you. I didn't realize how much until I lost you.
I made a stupid mistake. I slept with Cindy out
of anger and frustration. When you turned me
down, my ego took a beating and my hormones
were raging out of control. It happened right
after you turned me down. Cindy was there
convenient and easy."

Tamara got to her feet and moved away
from him. His confession didn't make it any
easier to hear.

"So because of raging teenage hormones
you put my life and yours in danger," she said
turning around to face him. "That's not love
Rodney. If you loved me, you wouldn't have
had sex with her. You would have waited until
I was ready. How could you not use protection
or did the condom tear again? How could you
put yourself and me at risk like that? How
could you not think with your head and not

another part of your anatomy? You knew about her reputation and you were still careless. Her reputation of being easy is the reason you slept with her."

He got to his feet and walked towards her. Tamara held up her hand to hold him at arms length.

"Tamara, I'm sorry. I'm not denying anything you said. I know you're right. I should have waited. I was a fool to mess around with Cindy or anyone else when I had you. I wasn't thinking straight and I blew it."

"Yes you did. We both did," she admitted. "I thought we had something special. I didn't know I was just another girl for you. I gave you the special gift of my virginity and you and I were both to young too appreciate it. It's something I can't take back. It's something I should have saved for the 'man' not the boy who was to be my husband, my soul mate. I'm sorry, but if you came here looking for forgiveness. I can't help you. I can't forgive you and I can't forgive myself."

"I don't know what I want or what I was expecting."

"I wasn't ready for this. I made love with you for all the wrong reasons. I did it to keep you from breaking up with me. I did it for you, not because it was something I wanted to do. It was a mistake Rodney. What if I had gotten pregnant? What would we have done? We were too young to make the decision to have sex. With sex comes consequences and look at us. We are not ready to face those consequences. The choices we make today affect us the rest of our lives. We both made bad choices. I should have waited. I let you manipulate me into bed when I knew I wasn't ready."

The backdoor opens and T.J. comes barreling into the house followed closely by her mother. Her mother smiles when she sees Rodney.

"Hello," she said walking further into the room. "I didn't realize you had company. I'm Mrs. Sims." Janet Sims holds out her hand to Rodney.

"Rodney Carter," he said hesitantly taking her outstretched hand.

Tamara watched the color leave her mother's face. She quickly recovered and glanced at her daughter.

"I'll take T.J. upstairs so the two of you can, finish your conversation. You're father is on his way home."

Her words left little doubt in Tamara's mind what she meant. She knew for his own safety he needed to be out of the house in the next half hour before her father came home.

"I listened to what you had to say and now I think you should leave. It's over between us. There is nothing left to say, but goodbye. Trust me when I say you don't want to be here when my father gets home."

Rodney said nothing as he walked out the door. Tamara sat down on the couch. Hugging the pillow to her chest, she closed her eyes and leaned back. She willed the phone to ring and put her out of her misery once and for all.

When the phone rang, she jumped and rushed to pick it up. Her hand shook as she brought the receiver to her ear.

"Hello," said the shaky voice. Her hand shook so badly she almost dropped the phone.

"I'm calling from Dr. Husbands office. May I speak with Tamara Sims."

"This is Tamara." Her eyes closed and she gripped the phone tightly. She said a silent prayer and took a deep calming breath. This was it. The waiting was finally over. This one conversation was about to change her life forever. Was she ready for the truth? Could she handle the truth? "Do you have the results of my blood test?"

Epilogue

Today the teen counseling center was packed with girls from all walks of life. They were there to hear the life stories of three very brave and courageous young girls.

Tamara, Alicia, and Rainey stood in the back of the room waiting to be introduced. Mrs. Sims signaled for them to come forward.

They nervously walked to the front of the room. Scanning the room, they were amazed at the turnout as the anxious girls waited for them to speak.

"I'm Tamara Sims. When my mother first approached us with the idea of speaking to you guys about what we've been through, we all turned tail and ran."

"I'm Alicia Perez and I'm pretty sure I ran the fastest," she admitted holding up her hand. "I wasn't ready to share what happened to me."

"My name is Rainey Michaels. We all ran, but we all came back. We each have a story to tell. It's not a particularly pretty story, but it's one we feel every teen should hear."

"We all belong to a club." Tamara held up her hand. "Before you get the wrong idea, it's not what you might think. It's not a country

club or a school club. This is a club we hope
many of you are not already a member of. It's
a club filled with guilt, pain and much regret."

"As part of my healing process," added
Alicia, "I'm standing here today."

"The name of our club is," they chorused
joining hands, "I Wish I Had Waited."

Printed in the United States
22264LVS00001B/61-102

9 780976 182900